THE ANUBIS TAPESTRY

THE ANUBIS
TAPESTRY

THIS BOOK
BELONGS TO:

The Anubis Tapestry:
Between Twilights

An ACTIONOPOLIS Book

KOMIKWERKS

Published by Komikwerks, LLC
1 Ruth Street
Worcester, MA 01602

Illustrations by Bruce Zick
Edited by Shannon Eric Denton
Book Design by Kristen Fitzner Denton
and Patrick Coyle

ISBN-13: 978-1490349756
ISBN-10: 1490349758

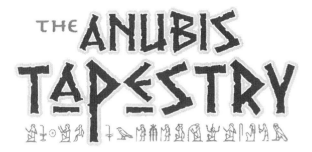

THE ANUBIS TAPESTRY

Between Twilights

Written and Illustrated
By Bruce Zick

Created by
Bruce Zick,
Shannon Eric Denton
and Patrick Coyle

ACTIONOPOLIS
When Adventure Is Your Destination!

TABLE
OF
CONTENTS

I was first wrapped in the magical world of Ray Harryhausen,

Then the Heka Magic was nutured by the tapestry of Jack Kirby.

And Finally, I was transported to the First Level of Beauty by the Love of Anja...

– Bruce

THE ANUBIS TAPESTRY

MAP OF THE UNDE
BOTTOMLESS PITS
THE RIFT
ETERNITY BRIDGE
RIVER OF SOULS
EARTH

RWORLD
RAZOR PEAKS
PORTAL
1
GUARDIAN
1
TO
LEVEL 2
PORTAL
2
TO
LEVEL 3
GUARDIAN
2
LEVEL 1
LEVEL 2
LEVEL 3
LEVEL 4
LEVEL 5
LEVEL 6
LEVEL 30
ANUBIS
LEVELS
7 - 29

PROLOGUE

There is the known Egyptian Mythology as written in the ancient texts and depicted in hieroglyphics.

And then there is what really happened...

The Portland Museum of Eastern Antiquities

CHAPTER ONE

It Started Out to be a Normal Day

I*t's was a perfect time to be outside,* Chance Henry thought. After weeks of rain, the sun had made a surprise appearance. All through the long school day, he had yearned to expose his pale skin to the sun and feel its heat on his face. Such was the reality of living in Portland, Oregon—when the sun came out you had better seize the opportunity. And now school was over, and Chance was ready for action.

In front of him, Holly Whipple dribbled the

basketball with ease, ready to embarrass Chance once again with her superior athletic skills. Why he had agreed to another humiliating game he could only guess; maybe he knew somewhere deep down inside that Holly liked being better than him at some things and proving it. And maybe he also understood that he enjoyed letting her have her way.

Just as Holly stepped forward, about to drive past Chance to the basket, he heard the one sound he always dreaded.

"Chance! Chance Henry! Come inside—I need your help."

"Sometimes," Holly said, "I think your dad doesn't want you to play after school at all."

Chance shrugged. "Yeah, you'd think. Well, duty calls. Tell the Horde I'll catch them later."

"At least you saved yourself from another sports embarrassment." Hasta Mañana." Holly spun the basketball on one finger, Globetrotter-style, then sank a perfect jump shot as Chance left the court.

He dragged himself down the street towards the Portland Museum of Eastern Antiquities. As the large building came into view, Chance noticed that its square brick front with small, narrow windows resembled a prison instead of a home. *Whoever heard of living in a museum anyway?* Chance entered the back apartment unit and trudged through the museum into the examining room. Sure enough, there was his father, Curator George Henry, surrounded by opened crates. Doctor Henry was bent over a new sarcophagus with a magnifying glass in hand. He looked up and smiled as Chance came over.

"Sorry to interrupt you, son, but I've got to prepare these new sarcophagi. This will be our greatest exhibit ever. Would you clear away the crate debris?"

"Sure dad, whatever you say."

Chance was pleased to see his father so happy. Ever since his mom died, things had been difficult. Doctor Henry tried to be a good father, but the responsibilities of doing everything himself were overwhelming at times. And Chance knew his dad worried about him. He desperately wanted to prove his self-reliance, but he didn't know how he'd ever get the opportunity, because his dad was so overprotective. Only recently had Chance won his long-running battle to be able to walk home from school instead of being picked up every day.

"I'm still amazed we have these new relics," his father commented as he continued working. "Of all the museums on the west coast, they chose us. I don't really understand it; we're such a small facility compared to Seattle or San Francisco. It's almost as if we were meant to have this exhibit."

"Yeah, it's weird, but in a good way, I guess." Chance carried an armload of wood debris to the corner.

"When you're finished, I'm going to need the large floor lamps." His father's attention was totally absorbed in the sarcophagus he was examining, and his tone was distant, as if he was talking to a lab assistant instead of his son.

Chance knew he wouldn't get back outside for

the rest of the day; this would go on all the way up to dinnertime. Yet another day spent indoors in the musty old museum instead of being with his friends. If his mom were still alive, he was sure

that she would insist that Chance be allowed to get out of the museum more often and have some fun.

Chance dragged the heavy lamp over to his dad and plugged it in.

"Isn't it a beauty?" Professor Henry asked. He held his magnifying glass over the tiny markings that had been carved along the side of the coffin thousands of years ago. Chance also studied the markings, interested in spite of himself.

“It looks like pre-third dynasty, if you ask me,” Chance said with authority.

George Henry paused in his study, then looked proudly at his son and smiled. “Very impressive, Chance. You know, you’re much smarter than I was at your age. When I was thirteen, all I cared about was comic books and baseball cards.”

Chance grinned back. “Well, I did have a good teacher.” He looked over the rest of the tomb, and noticed a small, square indentation about the size of his hand. “Hey, Dad, what’s this?”

Doctor Henry looked up for a moment. “That’s what was left of a storage compartment built into the coffin that often held jewelry or maybe even small canopic jars—you know, they contained dried body parts of the deceased. Looks like tomb raiders broke into both of these caskets. Whatever was in them is long gone by now, unfortunately."

"You know, I bet we could figure out the exact date." Chance started to get excited. "Who knows, it might be—"

Just then the light bulb in the floor lamp flared brightly, then went out with a pop.

"No problem, dad. I'll get another light from the warehouse." As Chance walked away, he heard his father muttering.

"When the Time of Anubis approaches," Dr. Henry translated from the Egyptian inscriptions, "the sons of Set and Osiris will rise from their sleep and walk in the future world." He adjusted the magnifying glass and carefully wiped away dirt with a soft small brush.

"Hmmm, there's a date mentioned here. Let's see…if my calculations are right, the Sons of Set and Osirius are to awaken… soon! Maybe in weeks, or even days. That's incredible."

Just as Chance stepped back into the room, fresh

light bulb in hand, bright golden light streamed out from under the sarcophagus lid.

"What is that?" Doctor Henry cried out, standing and dropping his tools. "Chance, stay back, something's happening!" His father tried to back away, but it looked like he couldn't move. Chance's breath caught in his throat, torn between wanting to help his dad and running for his life.

The sarcophagus lid opened.

When that happened, Chance tried to run for help, but his arms and legs had gone numb, paralyzed not with fear, but with a strange kind of power he felt radiating from the sarcophagus. Though he could barely move, he could see and hear. And what he saw was too incredible to believe.

A mummy stepped out of the ornate casket. It walked to the front of its tomb and growled, waving its wrapped arms in obvious rage. Chance saw it looking at the small indentation in the front of the sarcophagus. *It wants whatever had been in that compartment*, he thought.

The creature swung around towards Doctor Henry, its ancient bandages wiggling to life. They unwrapped from the mummy's withered body and waved in mid-air like the white tentacles of a

horrible beast, then flew over and wrapped around Chance's father.

Chance wanted to scream, but his throat had tightened so much that he could barely breathe. He watched the bandages squeeze into the very flesh of his father—into his face, his arms, his legs—like a second skin. His dad's features contorted into a face no longer recognizable. The remains of the mummy collapsed in a heap of sand. Chance's father no longer existed. In his place stood a completely different being. The creature that had taken over Chance's father touched his new face and laughed.

"After an eternity of waiting, I, Sehti, live again!! And now, the unlimited power and fury of the Underworld are mine for the taking. No one can stop me… except… Osirius. Unless he no longer lives."

Sehti suddenly bent over, his face twisting in pain as he grabbed his chest. "Uhhh, the transformation… like stabbing needles of fire!"

As Chance stood with his feet seemingly rooted to the floor, he noticed a glow in the room behind him. With an effort, he turned his head ever so slowly. To his horror, another sarcophagus was also glowing. As he watched, its lid scraped open, and another mummy slowly stepped out. It walked to the front of its crypt and examined the open secret compartment there. The mummy's featureless face swiveled over to look at Chance.

This can't be happening... this isn't real, Chance thought as a chill shot through his body. The hideous creature lumbered towards him, arms outstretched. Again Chance tried to run away, but his limbs refused to obey him. At the other sarcophagus, he saw Sehti straighten and walk toward him. Unable to move, Chance was trapped between two horrible, awful things from another time.

The hideous creature lumbered toward him

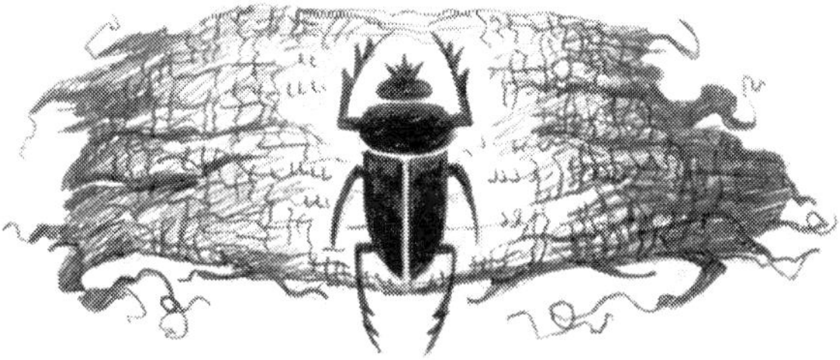

CHAPTER TWO

There are Good Mummies and there are Bad Mummies

The being that called himself Sehti frowned, its brow furrowing in thought as it regarded the boy. “The thoughts that once were a part of this body… they tell me, you are the son of… George Henry. You are… Chance Henry. You cannot be allowed to live!” Sehti’s pointed his outspread fingers at Chance and blue discs of light formed around his hands.

Chance heard words spoken behind him in

ancient Egyptian and looked over to see Osirius waving his linen-wrapped hands. As he finished speaking, shaft of blue light streaked across the room, seemingly straight at Chance! But the blue light flew just over his shoulder and struck Sehti, hurling him through the doorway. Osirius staggered backwards, collapsing against the side of his sarcophagus.

"How dare you strike me?" Sehti glared at Osirius. "I will send your feeble soul to the Land of Limbo." As Sehti waved his hands again he doubled over in agony. "Uhhh, using too much power… too soon after the transformation. Weak, so weak. Must regain my strength before exacting… my… revenge!"

Sehti limped across the museum floor to a back door, opened it, and stepped into the darkness.

Chance stared at Osirius. "Why did you… save… me?"

Osirius weakly lifted his hand and beckoned Chance to him. Knowing from his dad's research that the god Osirius was helpful to human, Chance hesitantly walked towards the mummy.

Osirius placed his hands on Chance's head. Instantly the magical mummy Tape began to unravel. Chance panicked, struggling to get free for a second.. Had he made a mistake in trusting the creature? Osirius bellowed a command and the Tape obeyed, rewrapping itself around the mummy.

Osirius stared deep into Chances eyes and he felt the mummy's vast, ancient consciousness probing his brain. Throughout it all Osirius kept chanting under his breath, gradually speaking more and more English.

"Thank you for trusting me, young man. My name is Osirius. Follow me if you want to live." He stood, swayed for a moment, and walked through the doorway, turning to glance back at Chance. "Well, don't just stand there gaping. Come on."

Chance lurched forward, almost falling over as his legs finally responded. "Wait a minute! What happened to my father?"

"Yes, your father—Doctor Henry. I saw

him in your mind, transformed by Sehti. I don't understand why my old friend has become evil. It was not our way, not the way of our sun god, Ra, to take another's life. The answer lies in the next room."

Osirius approached Sehti's sarcophagus and ran his hands across its surface. He noticed a small crack on the side of the crypt near the bottom of the casket.

"Ahhh, now I understand. Sehti's crypt must have been damaged centuries ago, letting in earthly oxygen that prevented him from a peaceful hibernation. My old friend…must have been driven insane by the awareness of the endless passage of time. What a waste." His head lowered, he breathed deeply. "Now I must face the danger of not only Anubis but Sehti as well."

Chance had heard enough. "Stop it! Stop talking! I don't care about anything except my father. What happened to him? We've got to help him… get him back!" Chance hunched over, sobbing as the realization of what had happened to his father hit him full force.

Osirius studied the boy. "How thoughtless of me. You are right to be upset. I'm sorry. No boy should see what you've seen. It is terrible. But if you want to help your father, you need to set aside your fear and listen to me, Chance Henry."

"I'm afraid your father, as you knew him, no longer exists," Osirius continued. "His body now belongs to Sehti, Disciple of Set. His essence—we call it his Ka—has been sent to the Land of Limbo, in the realm of the Underworld. But all is not lost, my young friend. There might be a way we can save him—if you are willing to help me."

"Me? Help you?" Chance whispered. "How could I… I… don't understand. What is Limbo?

And the Underworld? How can we save my father….?"

"So many questions, so hard to answer. If you will allow me, I will help you to understand." Osirius unwrapped a strand of Tape from his wrist and wound it around Chance's wrist. "This will be your first lesson in the use of what you mortals call… magic! Repeat after me. *Hp p kee n hrr-f n p-hw.*"

It sounded like a series of meaningless letters to Chance, but he didn't think he had anything to lose by trying. After several minutes, he spoke the phrase correctly. The Tape around his wrist glowed. The room swirled and faded away.

Osirius' booming voice echoed throughout the museum. "You now witness Egypt ten thousand years ago."

Whatever Osirius described, Chance saw. Hundreds, no thousands of people, all of whom lived and died many centuries ago in a civilization that had sprung from the basin of the Nile River. There before him were the all-powerful mythical

Old Ones, who led a struggling society of pre-Egyptians into a first Golden Age of the Nile. One day they realized it was time to leave Earth and make way for the New Age of Humanity. The mighty beings entered the Underworld, traveling through thirty portals across thirty levels, finally crossing through the Portal of Ra—to be gone for All Time's End to another dimension. They left behind them a whispering, slowly fading trace of their essence called the Vestige to guide humans safely towards a stable civilization.

The last Old One was named Anubis, the Boatman of the River of Souls, and was the Transporter of the Dead for Lord Osiris. He was instructed to follow the others after closing off the Underworld's entrance. But instead, he desired to reign supreme over all of Earth. He planned to sleep for many centuries until the Vestige had become so old and weak that it would completely vanish. Then nothing could challenge his power.

Anubis built a chamber on the thirtieth level, and, laying himself on an altar, he wove a powerful Heka Magick Spell. The entrance to the Underworld was sealed and hidden until the time neared for his Awakening. He drifted into sleep, across time, to awaken when the Vestige was gone—to awaken and return to become Lord of the Underworld, then step through the Rift and become Lord of the Upper World, Lord of All-Earth, Lord of this Universe.

Next, Chance saw Osirius and Sehti as strong, young men who were disciples of the Old Ones. These sorcerers, called the Magus, learned the ancient Art of the Heka… the Practice of Magika.

The Vestige commanded them to thwart the plans of Anubis by also sleeping until that dreadful time before the Awakening. The two men were sent to the Temple of Anubis where they found the magical Anubis Tapestry. Only the Anubis Tapestry had the power to locate Anubis in the secret 30th level of the Underworld and send him once and for all into the Great Beyond.

In a ceremony of mummification, the two men were wrapped in strands torn from the

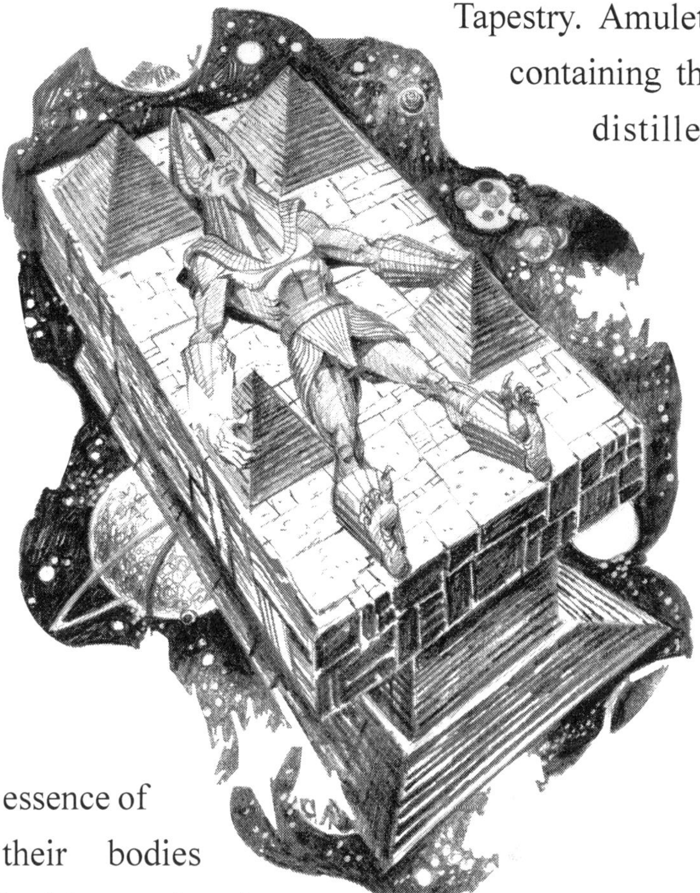

Tapestry. Amulets containing the distilled essence of their bodies had been placed in a secret compartment in the front of each sarcophagus. Once inside their crypts they slept while centuries passed. Chance saw the crack appear in Sehti's coffin, leaking in the air of mortal earth, which disturbed his sleep, eventually driving him mad.

The Vestige knew of the predetermined time and place where a Rift from the Underworld would open and allow Anubis to enter the modern world with his army of lost souls. The Vestige influenced the deeds of men over the ages so that the two sarcophagi would arrive at the correct time and place where the Rift would appear. Lastly, Chance saw the thieves his father had mentioned breaking into the sarcophagi. They stole the Amulets that could have restored the mummies' full powers. At that point, the vision faded and the room returned to normal.

Chance looked at Osirius anew and saw the goodness, the gentleness of the man who made the ultimate sacrifice. Chance actually felt sorry for him, for the loss of his family, to sleep for so many centuries, to become a mummy… part dead, part alive, and wake up in a world so unlike his own, which had now been lost for thousands of years.

"It was so real," Chance said, "like I was really there in the past. But… how…?"

"You keep the Tape around your wrist. It will help you understand all that has transpired. That is, if you don't mind. Allow me, as a token of our new friendship, to grant you a gift of magick from the Anubis Tapestry as meager compensation for your great loss"

"Well, okay… if it will help me get my dad back…"

Osirius smiled and nodded, as he spoke several words. The tape tightened against Chance's skin and became a continuous seamless strand.

"You have taken the first important step into the world of ancient magick we called Heka. You are officially a first level Magus. Congratulations, young man."

"Chance stared at the Tape, which now almost looked like a tattoo against the skin of his arm. "But how will this help us save my dad? You promised we could save him."

"And so we shall. We have three goals to accomplish. It is imperative that we stop Anubis from awakening, and we must also stop Sehti.

And most importantly for you, we shall save your father."

Chance felt like his head would explode from all the information he had seen and heard recently.

"I need your help," Osirius continued, "just as you need mine. Sehti has inhabited the healthy body of your father, so he is more powerful than I. Because I am sane, and refuse to destroy life to strengthen myself, I'm weaker and therefore at a disadvantage. But if you learn the art of Heka and become a Magus, the two of us together can defeat Sehti."

"Okay… I guess it all makes sense… sorta…" Chance said without much conviction. He wasn't sure, but he also thought he heard a faint humming in the back of his head, perhaps from the Tapestry, as if it was making him aware of things he couldn't consciously understand yet.

Osirius thought a moment, then stuck out his Tape-wrapped, white hand. "I believe you have a custom that concerns the shaking of two hands to symbolize partnership." He took Chance's hand in his and they shook hands awkwardly.

"And now, you must go to bed and get… a good night's… sleep. Tomorrow you will continue your schooling. We have to keep up appearances here and not break your routines, else we bring suspicion upon this place."

"Sleep?" Chance looked at the clock and realized how incredibly late it was. He could only guess that what seemed like minutes when Osirius showed him ancient Egypt was in fact hours, hours in which he might have actually traveled centuries backwards in time. Chance wasn't sure if he could fall asleep after what had happened. "I guess I'll try… umm… Goodnight, Osirius."

Osirius nodded. Chance thought he detected a slight smile through Osirius' bandages.

As Chance lay in bed, he wondered how he would ever get over losing his father. Sure, Osirius said they could save him, but Chance distrusted other adults besides his father. Hadn't they told him his mother was going to be okay when they knew she was terminally ill?

Chance thought about those awful moments when Sehti had turned his dad into that horrible creature. The memory of the Anubis Tape, like white snakes wiggling around Sehti's head, was terrifying. His heart raced. He must have been crazy to accept the Anubis Tapestry! Chance anxiously tried to pull it off, but it was like a second layer of skin. Somehow he had to get it off!

Just as Chance felt an overwhelming nausea flood his stomach, he saw symbols on the Anubis Tape glow and dance about his wrist. Strange little animals galloped in an endless circle on his arm. Elsewhere, wide oval eyes blinked, birds flew, and funny little people sat and prayed, or marched in single file.

Chance was mesmerized. He barely noticed that his fear was fading away. A moment later he yawned, then drifted into sleep—wonderful, delicious, glorious sleep…

As Chance drifted off to sleep, he didn't notice that his bedroom door was open just a crack, and the thin form of Osirius watched over him protectively as he drifted off. “Sleep, young warrior. Sleep and know a moment’s peace,” the mummy murmured as he shut the door.

Osirius sat at the dinette table

CHAPTER THREE

Blixx, Roxxx, and Goths

Chance awoke to a usual gray, dreary morning. As his eyes opened, he remembered the events of last night, and shook his head. "Wow, what a weird dream! Mummies—hah! Ridiculous."

As he sat up in bed, he saw his piece of Anubis Tape on his wrist, and reality crashed into him. It was real—terribly, sadly real. He stared at the little symbols and wondered if they would come alive again. He rubbed the Tape and waited, but nothing happened.

Chance reluctantly dragged himself out of bed,

washed up, dressed, and walked into the kitchen. Osirius sat at the dinette table looking even more weak and exhausted than he had the day before—he had probably been up all night. George Henry's papers, monthly bills, newspapers, correspondence, documents and photographs—all were strewn about the table. Osirius wearily rubbed his eyes. Chance noticed grains of sand leaking from the mummy's head.

"Good morning, Chance. As you can see, I've been studying all the bits and pieces of your father's life."

Chance nodded, grunted, and fixed a bowl of cereal. He thought how strange it was that a mummy, wrapped up in old stinky bandages, sat at his breakfast table—where his dad used to sit. Chance's mood changed from fascination to sadness.

"Are you sure we can save my father?"

"Yes, I believe we can. You must be patient and have… faith."

"I'm not very good at being patient," Chance

admitted. He watched Osirius rub his eyes again as more sand drifted to the tabletop. Chance left the room and a minute later he returned holding a pair of glasses.

"These are my dad's reading glasses. Maybe they'll help you."

Osirius tucked the ends of the glasses through the bandages on his head, and Chance smiled at the comical sight. The mummy looked at a document again.

"By the Art of Heka—it's a miracle! I can see clearly. Thank you, Chance."

"Oh yeah, sure. No problem."

"You know, in my prime I had the eyes of a hawk." Now… I have the eyes of a… mummy." Osirius sadly looked off into the distant place, lost in thought. Chance thought about saying something to reassure him, but nothing came to him at that moment. Then he noticed it was time to get going.

"Uh oh, I'm gonna be late for school. See you later, Osirius."

"Be sure to keep your sleeves buttoned down,"

Osirius said. "No one must see the Anubis Tape."

Outside the museum, Chance almost collided with Holly, who was waiting for him at his doorstep.

"Hey, watch it, Henry. You almost stepped on my new Adidas. What's the matter with you, did you sleep late dreaming about finally winning a basketball game or something?"

"Yeah, really funny, Hercules." Whenever Chance wanted to annoy Holly, he called her Hercules. Holly was just a little self-conscious of her slender, slightly muscular physique, but she was very pretty as well, though Chance would never tell her so.

"You wish you were half as strong as me, Henry." Holly never called Chance by his first name. "And what's this?" She brushed at his sleeve, sending bits of sand flying.

"Umm—I was helping my dad unpack some

relics for our exhibit, and some sand got on my clothes." Chance hoped Holly bought his fib, it was the best thing he could come up with on short notice. He thought she had, but as they walked to school, he felt her looking at him sideways during the entire trip.

Meanwhile, on the southern edge of town in an old abandoned industrial warehouse area along the Willamette River, Sehti slowly walked in the shadows. During the night, he had broken into a pawn shop and taken a long black leather trench coat to cover himself in the cool evening air.

Sehti approached an abandoned loading dock that was a temporary shelter for three teenagers. They wore black Goth clothing, and had tattoos, multiple piercings, and oily spiky hair. The group's leader looked at Sehti's bandages and smirked.

"Hey, man, you just get out from surgery? Do

Pulses of light shot out from Sehti's fingers

the doctors know you've left the building?" The teens laughed, amused by their cleverness. They surrounded Sehti.

The leader fingered the lapel of the leather coat. "Excellent threads, old man. I think it's just my style."

Sehti threw up his hands and howled a series of Heka Words of Power. Suddenly the wind roared. The bandages around Sehti's head loosened and danced in the air like snakes on Medusa's head. The three Goths drew back from him, fear on their pale, metal-adorned faces.

"You are sad, lost children. You need salvation. You need a lord, a master. You need Sehti! And Sehti needs an army of strong soldiers. The three of you are a good start."

Before the three teens could flee, blue oblong pulses of light shot out from Sehti's fingers, bathing all of them in bright beams. They hunched over in pain, and… growled! The humans transformed into something else, their skin turning tough and leathery, their eyes shining a bright green,

The banks of the Willamette River

their fingernails growing longer, their eyeteeth lengthening into fangs. They shuffled closer to their new master, whines and growls coming from their throats.

Sehti was pleased to see his powers slowly returning. Soon, all of his abilities would be rejuvenated and then…no living being on Earth could stop him. "Come with me, my soldiers. We have an empire to build!"

Sehti led his new followers along the banks of the Willamette River until they found an old abandoned logging mill that he deemed suitable. He kicked in the large metal door and regally entered his new domain. Waving his hands again, the Anubis Tape glowed and green spheres of light shot out of his fingertips, exploding in the air. Rusty old iron equipment groaned and twisted and contorted, standing on their metal legs, as they transmutated into massive braziers filled with leaping fire. Sehti smiled. With another sweep of his hands, huge old-growth timber posts blossomed into beautiful Egyptian lotus columns. The Magus turned to his children.

"Clean up this pig sty. Your new pharoah must have a suitable palace."

Back on the other side of the river, the longest Friday in Chance's life finally ended. Thank goodness it was now the weekend. As everyone poured out of Lincoln Jr. High School, Chance tried to leave unnoticed.

"Hey, Henry, what's the huge hurry?

He turned to see his three friends, Holly Whipple, Hayden Shaw, and Christi Hamilton. The four of them were the Horde. They had been friends for a long time before they realized that either their first or last name started with an H. This made them feel like their friendship was special, so they decided to use a variety of words that started with H in their conversations. Sometimes, like at this exact moment, Chance found this all a bit annoying.

"Oh, uhhh, I got some stuff to do at home," Chance explained. Gotta Haul."

"Okay, Henry, we'll see you tomorrow then," Christi said. "Hasta manana."

"Ummm, yeah… tomorrow— right. I… can't make it. Something really Hairy came up yesterday. I was gonna tell you at lunch, but, I… uhh, I forgot."

"No way, Hosehead." Hayden said. "We've been planning this weekend for months. You can't back out now!"

Chance's friends surrounded him. Holly grabbed Chance's wrist, the one with the Anubis Tape. "So, Henry… what's the story?" Chance felt the Anubis Tape heat up, the warmth spreading up his arm.

"Owww!" Holly cried out, instantly letting go. "You almost burned my hand. That was Harsh! How did you do that?"

"I… didn't do anything. Maybe you just got a hand cramp. I'm sorry guys, I've really got to get going." Chance took off down the street, feeling his friends watching him all the way down the block until he turned a corner.

As Chance arrived at the museum he wondered what Osirius had been doing all day. A sign hanging in the front lobby window read "Closed for Repairs." *Good idea. Osirius is pretty smart*, Chance thought as he walked around to the back apartment and began to unlock the door with his key.

"Who isssss itttt?" a strange voice asked from inside.

"You know who it is, it's me—Chance. Open up!"

"What'ssss the passsssword?"

"Password? There isn't any password. Osirius… is that you?"

"Oh yeah…da kid." The door slowly opened and a strange little head poked out. "Well… don't just stand there gawking! C'mon in."

"Who the… what in the heck are you?" Chance stared at a gnarly little two-legged creature with a snout and floppy ears that barely came up to his chest.

A gnarly, little, two-legged creature

"I'm Blixx, you moron. Get yer butt in here and close da door, fer cryin' out loud!"

"How did you get in here? Where's Osirius?"

"He's busy. And I'm busy—so don't bother us!" Blixx hopped up on the computer table, sat cross-legged, and began rapidly typing on the keyboard.

"WHERE IS OSIRIUS?" Chance shouted.

Just then another strange creature rushed into the room. This one was taller than Blixx, thin-bodied, with legs like a goat, long hairy monkey arms, and a cow-like face. And it wore a kitchen apron.

"Shhhh!" the cow-creature said. "Osirius is concentrating. Don't make such a racket!"

"Who are you?" Chance felt like he was having a nightmare.

"I'm Bluthher, young man. Have you had something to eat yet? You look absolutely famished. Oh my… look how skinny you are!"

"What's going on around here? I'm going to find Osirius!"

"I don't know how I'm sssupposed to get any work done wit all disss racket," Blixx said as he looked up from the computer. "I've got a lot to learn about dis century, and there ain't no time ta do it." Chance was about to start yelling again when Blixx stood. "All right, little Henry, shut yer trap, ya made yer point. Foller me. I'll take you to da bossss."

Seething, Chance followed Blixx through the museum to the warehouse,where Osirius sat hunched over a long metal table busily carving a small object. He wore a long sleeved pinstriped shirt and slippers, and his new glasses.

"Osirius, what's going on around here? Where did these creatures come from? And is that my dad's shirt?"

"Shhh. A moment, please! I'm in the middle of something very important. Almost done. Alllmmmmmoossssttttt donnnnne. There! It's finished." Osirius looked up proudly. "As you know, Chance, as long as Sehti is out there somewhere, we are extremely vulnerable here. I placed a Heka Formulae around the entire museum for safety's sake, but we need more security. We need the Roxxx."

"Rocks?" Chance looked puzzled.

"No, Chance. Not rocks. Roxxx."

"That's what I said…rocks," Chance snapped.

"No no. I'm not saying the noun "rocks, I'm saying the name "Roxxx."

"You're saying the same thing twice," Chance cried out! "This is all too crazy.

"SHHHHH!" both Osirius and Blixx said simultaneously.

"And we were having such a peaccceful day… until now," Blixx added.

Chance, more curious now than mad, walked over and saw that Osirius had been carving an eight inch piece of granite into something that looked like a creepy little golem.

"Young man, this will be your first lesson in the Art of Heka Magick. You see, in my world, we used Words of Power, images or Symbols of Power and objects, or Figures of Power."

"Uh oh. I feel like I'm back in school."

"In a way you are, so please pay attention. I'll try to make this easy. If we write the word for bird, it is more than a word, it really is a bird. If we speak that word, then a bird will appear. If we carve an image of the bird, that image really is a bird. I have here a Figure of Power in the shape of a Roxxx. You and I will now say the ancient Word of Power for Roxxx. Repeat after me—*te-f hrre.t n nb gbe-t.*"

Chance tried very hard to repeat the phrase, but the syllables kept tripping over his tongue, and vice versa. Osirius corrected him twenty-seven times before he spoke the ancient words accurately.

"Very good. Now, stand back, Chance." Osirius placed the statue on the floor, stepped back and waved his hands, his pinky fingers bent forwards. A blue disc of light formed around each pinky. Then a thin strand of light connected the two discs together. From the center of the strand, a third, smaller disc of light appeared. A larger burst of light shot out and struck the granite Figure of Power.

The stone golem glowed and vibrated. It grew slowly at first, then faster until it reached a height of nine feet! Suddenly its eyes opened wide!

The Roxxx slowly took a step forward, then another, making a loud scraping sound of stones grinding against each other. The giant walked to the center of the room and slowly looked in all directions, as if it could see everything not only in the museum, but also for miles around them. Then the Roxxx stood completely still and shut its eyes. It no longer looked alive.

"We are safe now, Chance. The Roxxx will remain on guard, and not move again unless we ask it to, or unless we are in danger. The Roxxx will protect us."

"B.... butt how can it be alive…it's…he's solid granite. That's…amazing! Wow! But, I don't like the name Roxxx—it's too much like rocks. Hmmm, he's granite, right? I'll call him… Grant."

"Grant?" Osirius searched for a connection. "Yes…I understand. Granite—Grant. Hahhaha. That's funny, isn't it? A play on…English words.

Then the Roxxx stood completely still

Grant! Yes, well done, Chance. Grant it is."

Chance was surprised to hear Osirius laugh. He had seen many mummy movies, and he had just assumed they didn't have a sense of humor. He smiled too, until he saw Osirius lean against the worktable, his head sagging. Chance and Blixx rushed to help him sit down. A large pile of sand drifted to the floor. Blixx frantically massaged Osirius' neck and shoulders, accidentally releasing more sand. "You do too much, masssster. You mussst resssst now."

"I forgot that I'm no longer at full strength." Osirius took a few deep breaths, his eyes wincing in pain. "To make such a powerful servant required some of my own life's energy. Even at full strength I could only create one such creature."

"Is there anything I can get you?" Chance asked. "Some aspirin? Maybe you need to eat something. Uhhh, you do eat, don't you? Is everything inside you… uh, does it all work, you know? I mean, you are… umm, well… are you alive?"

"Yes, you can be quite assured that I am

fully alive," Osirius said with a smile. "Once my sarcophagus opened, I was essentially re-animated by the Magick of Heka. Oh, I'm quite old and… well, shriveled—but I can assure you, I'm not dead…yet. Yes, I think a meal would be a good idea. Let's see what Bluthher can create for us."

As Blixx helped Osirius out of the warehouse, Chance glanced back at the frozen granite hulk. He did feel safer now, but at the same time was alarmed at how his world was changing so dramatically. *Is life ever going to be normal again?*

Chance wondered if they might ever need the protection of Grant. He tried to imagine the huge rock creature springing into action, all that terrible, awesome strength unleashed. Grant looked like nothing in the world could hurt him. He shuddered at the thought—here in his home, stood some... *thing* that might represent… total destruction!

Chance trembled, and hurried to catch up with Osirius and Blixx.

Bluthher busily cooked dinner

CHAPTER FOUR

The Bad News Keeps Getting Worse

"We mussst eat, we mussst eat. We are hungry, yes? Follow meeee." Blixx led Osirius and Chance through the museum to the back apartment.

"So, Osirius, who are these guys?" Chance asked.

"We call them Mythixx. Blixx is the last of a race of Ihhmphs, and Bluthher, well… Bluthher is… unique. There was a tradition in the Old

Times; when we were mummified, our servants accompanied us on our journey to the Underworld. Blixx was Sehti's assistant and Bluthher served me. Sehti and I transformed Blixx and Bluthher into Symbols of Power that were carved into our sarcophagi. I simply restored them today while you were at school. They are very handy, don't you think?"

Chance wrinkled his nose. "Ummm, yeah, but they do kind of stink." It was true—Blixx smelled like a wet dog, and Bluthher's odor reminded Chance of a moldy bathroom.

But as they stepped into the kitchen, Chance was amazed at how good the cooking smelled. He and Osirius sat at the kitchen table and Blixx hopped back up on the side table to continue surfing the Internet.

"Did you place those orders we discussed, Blixx?" Osirius asked.

"Yesss. Ohh yesss, Master. This In..ter…net is amazzzzing. You can get anything in de world delivered to yer home. There are da cutest little toy goblins with long hair that...."

"I trust that you will refrain from any unnecessary purchases?" Osirius said sternly.

"Yeah... I uh... I knew that." Blixx looked at his new master guiltily, and Chance made a note to keep an eye on the little creature. After all, he knew that look—it was the one he gave his father whenever he was going to try to do something without permission.

Meanwhile, as Bluthher finished preparing dinner, Chance tried to figure out if the tall, gangly being was male or female. There was something very motherly about its relationship with Chance and the others, so he decided that Bluthher was a female.

"How do you know to work the stove?" he asked her.

"Ohh, that... Osirius imparted the necessary information to us when he gave us life. And cooking itself is al in the spice." She turned a sizzling, pink salmon fillet in the pan. "That's also how Blixx uses your in—ter—net."

Chance nodded. "Of course." *Hey, after everything else that's happened, why can't a cow-headed monkey-goat whip up a delicious-smelling meal on our stove?* he thought.

"This is my plan, Osirius suddenly declared. "As I said earlier, I need your help to defeat Sehti and Anubis. You must learn the Art of Heka and become a powerful Magus."

"Me… become a powerful Magus?" Chance's eyes widened.

"Oh yes," Osirius said. "You have abilities you've never known existed. I will teach you how to tap into your strengths. Also, you have a special advantage no one else on this planet has."

"I'm… not sure I understand. I'm just an ordinary…"

"You are not ordinary," Osirius interrupted. "You are unique. The blood that runs through your veins also runs in Sehti's, since he now occupies your father's body. The two of you have a special bond that will always protect you. The laws of the Magi forbid taking the life of your own blood-kin, so Sehti would not dare kill you, at least not directly."

Chance brightened. "Wow, that's the best news I've had in days. You don't know how much I've worried that…"

"Understand this, Chance. Sehti can still harm you. He can take indirect action against you that could lead to your death. I'm simply saying he cannot directly attack you."

"Ohh. That's not what I thought you said." Chance felt more hopeless now. He was just a kid, yet Osirius expected him to face off against a sorcerer who was thousands of years old?

"You do have another advantage, my friend. Because of the blood kinship you can also be trained to hear Sehti's thoughts. I will teach these abilities to you… in time. But there is only one way you can become so powerful."

Chance leaned forward, simultaneously dreading and eager to hear the next words. He knew he would need all the help he could get. But it seemed that everything associated with the mummies came with a price, like the complete upheaval of his former life—and he wasn't sure he wanted to keep paying.

"Chance Henry—you must wear all of the Anubis Tape. With that and Heka Amulets and Bracelets, you will be a mighty warrior. You must become… a mummy!"

A cold wave of horror washed over Chance. "You mean become something like you? No Osirius, there's got to be another way! I'm not going to become some sort of freak. NO WAY!"

Osirius took a deep breath. "I'm sorry, Chance, but there is no other way to save your father. You must not let your fear control you."

"But… I don't want to be a mummy." Chance paused. "I can't even believe I'm saying that."

"We will be able to keep your transformation a secret, hidden under your clothes. You must prepare yourself for a long hard struggle, my boy. It will take months to learn the way of Heka Magick, maybe longer. And we must not forget that Sehti grows stronger every day. If we do not increase our combined strength soon, we will not be able to stop him."

Chance walked over to the window, and looked outside at the normal street, normal cars, normal people walking around. As if he didn't already feel like he had little, if any control over his life, now he was going to lose control over his own body. Could it get any worse than this? But, if it meant saving his father... *What choice do I have?*

He turned back to the mummy. "Okay, Osirius. Okay. I'll do it."

"I sssalute you, young sssir," Blixx said, raising his spindly fingers to his brow. "You are brave beyond your yearsss. You will make a great warrior, and a great Magus. Maybe the greatessst that ever wasss. You will seeeee! You will sssave yer father, yessss you will."

Osirius gave Blixx an annoyed look. Blixx heard the telepathic voice of Osirius. *"There will be no further mention of Chance saving his father. There are many secrets yet untold that Chance is not ready to hear, so we must not falsely build up his hopes."* Blixx nodded to Osirius, who very slightly nodded back.

Chance wondered what had just happened, but then Bluthher announced that dinner was ready, and Chance forgot all about the strange looks between the other two when his stomach rumbled loudly.

After a delicious meal of blackened salmon, sautéed spinach and kale, and wild rice with parsley and almonds, Chance and Osirius returned to the warehouse. Chance stared at Grant, but he didn't see any signs of movement. Osirius waved Chance over to the table next to him.

"We have much work to be done. I want to be

absolutely sure you will be as protected as possible when you journey to the Underworld."

"Underworld?!" Chance felt the wonderful meal he had just eaten lurch in his stomach. "Nobody said anything about me going to the Underworld."

"Young man, there is only so much I can tell you at any given time. I want you to learn slowly so that you understand each and every thing I impart to you. Yes, you must go to the Underworld if you are to save your father. I am too weak for such a journey, and I will not take a life as Sehti did in order to increase my strength. It must be you, and it is my responsibility to prepare you."

"This just gets better and better. All right, Osirius, tell me about… the Underworld." Chance braced himself for even more distress.

"The Underworld was where the dead all first traveled before they found their final resting place, until it was sealed off by Anubis. The only way into it is through the Rift that will appear only on the first night of each new moon, between Twilights."

"It is a great privilege to wear the Anubis Tape," Osirius said as he peeled another piece of the Anubis Tapestry from his forearm. "Never before has such a wondrous thing been made on Earth. Why, the Old Ones themselves infused it with their very life essence."

Osirius wrapped the tape around Chance's forearm. The new bandage tightened around Chance's forearm and magically sealed together. Osirius peeled off another length of tape and also wrapped that onto Chance's arm. Then finally a last length was applied. Osirius' withered, stick-like arm was now bare, and Chance's arm was completely covered.

"And now, Chance, we shall create our first Amulet. When it is wrapped around your arm, you will have complete control over the Anubis Tape."

As Osirius reached to pick up a piece of marble, he paused at the sight of his own exposed arm. Osirius dreaded the removal of all the Anubis Tape that must be worn one day by Chance. It would be painful to loose the Heka Magick of the Anubis Tapestry that helped his aged body withstand the ravages of time. He would dry up like millions of grains of sand that could hold no form, to disappear forever from this mortal world.

That was another secret he dared not tell Chance.

Osirius showed Chance the Symbols and Words of Power to carve in the marble that would become the Amulet. Chance took to the carving better than either of them had expected. Before he knew it, the mummy noticed that it was too late to continue the lessons, and he insisted that Chance go to bed.

But, as Chance lay awake in his room, he worried about his journey to the Underworld. Then his thought about becoming a mummy! What would it be like to be completely covered in the Anubis Tapestry? Would he still be human? Like an image from an old horror movie, Chance saw himself as The Mummy, slowly, awkwardly walking stiff-legged, arms outstretched, moaning and groaning, chasing fleeing citizens down the Portland streets.

The Tape on his forearm glowed slightly.

Chance stared at the numerous Symbols and Words of Power, waiting to see if they would move again as they did last night. He slowly drifted into sleep, his last thoughts returning to the Underworld… and of the dark journey that stretched out before him.

Sehti waved his hands over the brazier

CHAPTER FIVE

One Must be Very Careful to Use Correct Heka Pronunciation

While Chance fitfully slept, Sehti finished transforming the abandoned mill into an Egyptian palace. Thirty lotus columns in two long rows now towered over fifteen flaming braziers. The floors were made of marble inlaid with lapis lazuli and jade. Painted murals of the Nile River adorned the walls. At the end of the room, the floor rose in a series of wide steps to a magnificent throne of gold and silver. In the center of the room stood one huge flaming brazier.

Sehti waved his hands over the brazier and spoke Words of Power. With each new phrase, fiery flames of red and green licked higher, illuminating his ever-growing army of ten Goth-Beasts. Inside the flames, the streets of Portland appeared.

"Tomorrow is the night of the new moon," Sehti thundered. "It is so written that between Twilights, a Rift will appear, and through such a Rift may one gain access to the Underworld. I command the Flames of Fortune to show me the way. Reveal the path to my destiny so that I may find Anubis, who sleeps in his chamber on the thirtieth level."

Sehti beckoned the flames to rise higher. The Goth-Beasts recoiled in whimpering fear to the safety of the shadows.

"Though Anubis be fearsome and mighty, I shall defeat him. Though Anubis defied the Old Ones, though Anubis could destroy us with the merest flick of his finger…now he sleeps. And as long as he sleeps he is helpless. I will find you, Anubis, and destroy you. And then I will rule all existence, both here and in the Underworld."

Within the flames a dark and lonely street in Portland's Old Town appeared. In the middle of the street a shimmering Rift formed.

"There it is—the opening to the Underworld! There is my path, there lie my fortune and my future."

Sehti knelt before the fiery brazier and prayed.

Elsewhere, George Henry called out through the mist of the Underworld.

"Chance… Chance, where are you? Help me, son. Hellpppp meeee!"

Wailing winds blew across the blackened, twisted, desolate rock landscape, whipping up a sand storm that stung him. George Henry stumbled and fell to the harsh ground, blindly reached out, groping the air for a helping hand.

"Chance…. Chance…. Chance…" His words grew softer; his form faded in the obliterating sand.

Then all was blackness.

It was the worst nightmare of Chance's life. He woke up drenched in sweat, his father's voice still echoing in his head.

The next morning, Chance was still shaken by his dream as he walked into the kitchen. A strange man was setting several packages onto the table.

"Who are you?" Chance shouted. "How did you get in here?"

The man held up his hands in a calming gesture. "It's me, Osirius. I cast a Heka Formulae to hide my form. I'm sorry I alarmed you, but I had to receive these deliveries."

"Well, I don't like it. I was getting used to you the other way. Please, change yourself back."

"But of course…as you wish, although I might need my disguise from time to time." Osirius changed back to his mummy form.

"Come and eat your breakfast," Bluthher implored. "Chance did you shower? Are you wearing clean socks? Come come. Sit down and eat before it gets cold."

They sat down. Chance noticed that the kitchen was sparkling clean and bright. Bluthher delivered plates of poached eggs with hollandaise sauce, sausage links, and toast with raspberry jam. As Chance tore into his wonderful breakfast he realized that Bluthher was standing to his side. He looked up at her. She raised an eyebrow expectantly. He instantly understood that she was in need of…a compliment.

"Bluthher, this is awesome. I don't know how you do it."

Bluthher looked slightly embarrassed. She picked up the corner of her apron and rubbed Chance's cheek. "I think you missed a spot when you washed your face. Chance, you did wash your face, didn't you?"

"Yes, mother," Chance joked. It was the first time he'd made a joke like this in a long time.

"Osirius," Chance asked, "do you…?" He stopped in mid sentence. "You know, it's hard to keep saying your name all the time—too many syllables. Would you mind if I called you, ummm… Cyrus? Or… Uncle Cy?"

"Chance, I'm flattered that you would consider me as your relative. Along that line of thinking, we should tell anyone who asks, that Professor Henry has gone on an expedition in Egypt. As your Uncle Cyrus, I will be your guardian in the meantime."

"Yeah, sure…that makes sense." Chance instantly lost his cheerful mood at the mention of his father being gone.

After breakfast, they returned to the warehouse with the new shipment of packages. Chance walked around Grant, looking for any scuffmarks on the floor by his feet. There were no telltale signs of movement.

Cyrus noticed his examination of the stone

creature. "Do not worry, Chance. Grant will let us know the instant there is danger."

"Yeah, that's kind of what I'm afraid of," Chance replied as he went back to the table and began helping the mummy.

At the table, Uncle Cyrus unwrapped the many contents from the packages. With great ceremony, Cyrus placed the marble piece Chance had carved onto a sheet of papyrus. They put a stick of olive wood under the papyrus, then sprinkled myrrh and kyphr and cinnamon on top. They next recited many Words of Power. When the marble object glowed, Uncle Cyrus

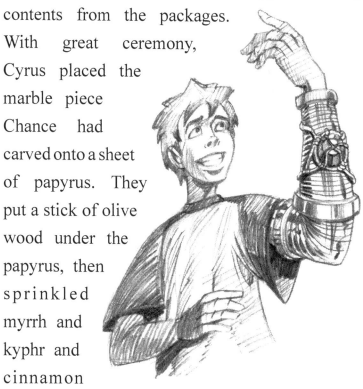

seemed satisfied. He taught Chance how to wrap and twist a thin silver wire around the stone. Finally the Amulet was complete and with an additional length of silver, it was wrapped around Chance's forearm.

Several more Words of Power were solemnly spoken. The Amulet glowed a pale green color. Suddenly the Anubis Tape quivered and then melded together into a hardened, seamless outer skin that resembled a layer of armor.

"Hey, that's really cool. It feels kinda heavy, like metal." Chance held up his arm and admired the Amulet.

"Every time you recite a Heka Formulae of Power, the Anubis Tape will thusly transform. Now I will teach you your first important Formulae." Uncle Cyrus escorted Chance to a corner of the warehouse.

"Point your right hand at that electric fan. Now, repeat after me: *'o-t n hmt n 'rq-hh n ntr-w nt n t p-t se'm-n.*"

Fifteen minutes passed before Chance

pronounced the sequence correctly.

As soon as the last letter was recited, a purple mist formed around Chance's forearm that rose and turned into a flat disc. Then a second disc formed above the first, then a third over the second, finally a fourth smaller purple disc formed over the third. A purple thread pierced through all four discs and at the upper end a large bubble the size of a soccer ball formed. The purple bubble flew away from Chance's arm and struck the fan. The fan blades stopped moving for three seconds.

"Whoa," Chance gasped. "That was awesome!"

"Now, my young Magus, we shall transfer Anubis Tape from my right arm to yours." Cyrus slowly unwrapped each length of bandage and wrapped the Tape around Chance's right arm, this time all the way up to his armpit.

Chance had not reacted badly to his left forearm being bandaged, but as his right arm was taped, a sinking feeling of unreality grew more intense, as if he was no longer himself. Bit by bit, he really was being turned into a mummy! For a moment, he desperately wanted to tear off the Anubis Tape and run as fast as he could. But Chance remembered his father, trapped in Limbo, and gritted his teeth until the wrapping was complete.

"There," Cyrus said. "We're done. If we have time we'll make another Amulet, and a Bracelet as well. But I have many things to teach you before your journey. It is extremely important that you recite the exact pronunciation of each Formulae. You must practice them as much as possible. I will only teach you a few today; that is all you could possibly remember. Now we must work on a lasting immobility spell. Repeat after me: *n nhe ntei-k mt-t ar-f n sp m-mne.*"

After thirty minutes of practice, Chance was able to correctly recite the Formulae. The mummy told him to repeat the Formulae while pointing his hands at the fan again. Chance began, but as he spoke the *"mt-t"*...

"NO—you mispronounced it!!" Cyrus shouted.

Chance's world turned upside down.

The room became a strange alien dimension

A horrible beast of black tar and slime and dirt

of roiling mist. Chance saw Sehti standing in the middle of a line of semi-human creatures in black leather. The transformed mummy was staring down into a blazing fire. Slowly his head lifted and he stared straight at Chance.

"Son of George Henry—you are a fool, a child playing in a world you can't possible understand. I can feel your fear, your doubts. You will not escape me. And do not believe for one second that you will ever save your father."

Sehti's form slowly dissolved. Then Chance saw a new shape that his mind told him was the thirtieth portal of the Underworld. A horrible beast of black tar and slime and dirt guarded the opening. It had huge dripping fangs and seven horns rose from its lumpy skull. Chance felt himself fly through the portal into the very Chamber of Anubis, where the god lay asleep atop a large stone slab. The Old One's eyes snapped open and Chance fell through its green pupils into a dimension where Anubis stood in all of his terrible glory.

Here was mighty Anubis, king of the

Here was mighty Anubis

Underworld. He opened his taloned fingers and all the monsters, all the demons, all the tormented souls of the Land of the Lost spilled forth, growing into a fearsome Army of the Damned. Anubis mouth open wide, then impossibly wider still, howling an ear splitting shriek that would most certainly drive Chance mad within moments.

Suddenly Chance was back in the warehouse. Cyrus bent over him, repeating a mantra of Words of Power until he was sure Chance was all right. "It's over now, Chance. You're safe. Everything is okay."

"Cyrus, I saw Sehti, but then I think I was in the Underworld. Anubis was there and he was so powerful, so frightening. It was awful."

"You had a vision caused when you mispronounced the Formulae. But it wasn't real. What you saw was a product of your own fears. You mustn't be afraid, Chance. You are very strong and resourceful. I will try my very best to protect you."

Chance shook his head. "It's too much, Uncle

Cy. I was wrong—about everything. I can't do this. I don't have any control. I can't go to the Underworld. I can't.... I can't. I... I've got to get out of here."

Chance bolted out of the room before Cyrus could stop him.

Blixx watched though the back door window

CHAPTER SIX

Talismans, Amulets, Monsters and… Duct Tape

Chance sat slumped on the back door step. Minutes before, he had run as fast as he could, as far away as he could, from Osirius and the museum. But eventually, he realized he had no idea where he was going. Once he stopped to catch his breath it became obvious that the answers to his problems were back inside the museum, the very place he was trying to escape from. Now he was back where he had started, and still no closer to knowing what he should do. Then Chance heard voices. Looking up, he saw Holly, Christi, and Hayde.

"Hey, I thought you had to go somewhere," Holly said with a frown. "And here you are, just hanging at home. This is really Hostile."

The last thing Chance wanted just then was to deal with the Horde. He walked towards them, wishing he was anywhere else but here at the moment.

"Yeah, well, I was supposed to go over to my relatives, but they called up and… my cousin got sick… so we didn't end up going. I was…gonna call you guys, but, uhhh…then my Uncle Cyrus stopped by and…"

"Nice story, Henry," Hayden sneered, "but we aren't buying it."

While they talked, Chance saw Blixx poke his head up to watch through the back door window. Holly noticed the movement too and looked at the back door just as Blixx ducked out of sight.

"What was that?" Holly cried out. "I though I

saw something weird."

"Uh..." Chance welcomed a change of topic. "...maybe a monster or something, huh Holly? Maybe you saw a ghost."

Hayden poked Chance in the chest. "You're really blowing us off, aren't you? Okay, we can take a hint. Hasta la vista, Henry." The three turned and walked off.

Chance wanted to call them back, he wanted so badly to tell them what was going on, but he was sure they wouldn't believe it. Shoot, even he had a hard time believing it. But it was happening. And if the only way to save his dad was to become a mummy—*but how am I going to stop Sehti, mummy or not? There's no way.*

Chance heaved a deep sigh and turned around, trudging back to the museum. What he didn't see was Holly looking back at him, a worried expression on her face.

During the rest of the day, Cyrus taught Chance only a few Heka Formulae. But Chance was distracted and unable to concentrate—too worried about the hopeless quest he was about to go on. Cyrus explained that tonight was a new moon and a Rift might open to the Underworld. If that were true, Sehti would be there. Chance shrugged at the news. *Even with Cyrus's help, I'm never going to be able to pull this off.*

Finally it was time for dinner and Chance wearily dragged himself back to the apartment.

After the meal, Cyrus entered the Egyptian artifact section of the museum. Feeling comfortable surrounded by objects from his homeland, he sat on the floor and placed a miniature granite pyramid in front of him. The Pyramid of Power glowed as Cyrus chanted Words of Power. It spun slowly, rising three feet above the floor and growing many times in size. Osirius felt the winds of the Nile, heard the giant palms sway in the breeze, smelled the sultry fragrance of the lotus flowers, and as tears formed in his eyes, he saw the dunes of the desert rise and fall like waves of the sea. Gradually the voice of the Vestige whispered through the Ether. But it was so faint. Its time had nearly passed.

"We hear you, oh faithful servant of Osiris. You have done well to survive the long journey through time. And now you are at a critical juncture of momentous forces. Tonight is the new moon; tonight appears the Rift. You must journey to the Netherworld and seek the domain of Anubis who still sleeps."

Just then Cyrus heard a knock at the front door of the museum. He snapped out of his trance, changed into his human appearance, and walked over and opened the door.

"Hello. Can I help you?" Cyrus asked.

A middle-aged woman looked at Cyrus suspiciously. An athletic-looking teenager about Chance's age stood by her side.

"Is Dr. Henry in?" Mrs. Whipple asked.

"No, I'm sorry, he isn't. Perhaps I can be of assistance." Cyrus bowed slightly.

"I'm Carrie Whipple and this is my daughter Holly. She's concerned about Chance and insisted I check in on him." She looked Cyrus up and down. "And you are…?"

"Oh, please forgive me. I'm Chance's Uncle Cyrus. I'm looking after him while George is away."

"I don't buy any of this," Holly interrupted. "Where is Chance?" Then she shouted, "CHANCE… ARE YOU OKAY?"

Suddenly Chance appeared next to Cyrus. "Yeah, duh—I told you I'm okay. Are you okay?" He turned to Cyrus. "I'll take care of this, Uncle Cyrus."

"Chance… Are you all right?" Mrs. Whipple asked.

"Sure I'm okay. Holly's just mad because I didn't hang out with the Horde today." He turned to Holly. "I appreciate you being worried, but my Uncle and I were in the middle of dinner and then we have a lot to do tonight. I'll talk to you later."

"I'm sorry we bothered you," Mrs. Whipple said, relaxing. "Come on, Holly."

"Thanks for checking in, Mrs. Whipple." Chance added. See ya."

Cyrus closed the door, but peeked out through a side window in time to see Holly look back at the building with a frown. *It is good that Chance has such concerned friends,* Cyrus thought, *but even they cannot help him in what he has to do now.*

Later, back in the warehouse, the storm that had been building inside Chance exploded.

"I can't go to the Underworld, Uncle Cy. I'm not strong enough, and I can't remember the Heka Formulae. What if I screw up? Who will save my

dad? Are you sure you can't come with me?"

Cyrus shook his head wearily. I'm afraid I cannot, Chance, I have already overextended myself recently, and the strain of crossing the dimensions would be too great for this body. However, it might help you to know that I'm sending Blixx with you. He has a perfect memory which will guarantee that you find your way back home." Blixx straightened and lifted his head proudly.

"Blixx?" Chance said, scornfully. "But, Blixx—don't take this the wrong way—he's a bit of a… goofball. And… he was Sehti's servant, right? So, how can we trust him? And how will he help me cast the right Formulae?"

"I'm not sure you understand what is at stake," Cyrus explained. "Sehti must not be allowed to find the Chamber of Anubis. But there's something else. Your father's Ka, his very soul, is there somewhere in the Underworld, but it will soon fade away. If you do not bring the Ka back tonight we will never be able to save George Henry. "

"Tonight!? Umm… I didn't know. Geez, do you ever have any good news for me?" Chance's fears were momentarily overshadowed by this new urgency. He straightened up and stared at Cyrus. "Then, I guess it's what I have to do. Okay… I'll do it!"

"Bravo, young hero," Blixx said. "You have again impresssed me. And do not worry. Now that Sehti is evil, I only serve Osirius and the forces of Good."

"Yeah, but I still think we're going on a suicide mission. Okay, Blixx," Chance said. "I guess it's just you and me. The two of us against the whole Underworld. Should be a piece of cake."

Cyrus admired Chance's effort to be humorous in spite of his fears. He pulled a six-inch tall carved statue out of his apron pocket and handed it to Chance, whose eyes widened when he saw it.

"It looks like… my dad! Cyrus—what…?"

"I have made a Talisman for you. When you find your father's Ka and recite a special Formulae, your father's spirit will be drawn into this totem. You will then be able to bring him safely back to our world." But it won't be easy to find his Ka. It drifts along the winds of Limbo. You will have to reach out and search for him with your mind, and even then, his spirit might be too difficult to find."

Chance touched the Talisman lightly. "I'll find him—I promise."

"Now," Cyrus said, "here's what you will find when you step through the Rift. In order to go from one level to the next, you must pass through a portal. Thirty levels, thirty portals. Each portal is guarded by a monster that you must conquer through trickery or Heka Magick. Once a monster is defeated, you will forever be its master."

"Monsters? Great. So now there's also monsters to worry about. Tell me it doesn't get any worse than this."

"Don't worry, young Magus" Blixx proclaimed. "You will have me by yer sssside."

"Gee, I feel better already."

"Listen closely, Chance," Cyrus continued. "I want you to follow Sehti from a safe distance. Watch him and learn—he is a wise traveler of the unknown. I will teach you one last Formulae that will change your appearance into a large rock. Oh, and be sure the two of you stand close together when you cast this one, otherwise it won't affect both.

"I think I'm starting to feel a little better now," Chance said. "And I'm glad Blixx is going with me. But—is there any way I can talk to you from the Underworld?"

"In a manner of speaking. I will be able to communicate to you through Blixx because he is a creature of magical origins."

Cyrus spent the next hour teaching Chance the last Formulae. Then Cyrus handed him a tiny Hourglass.

"This Heka Hourglass will keep track of the time that passes between Twilights. You must return through the Rift before the last grain of sand falls into the lower chamber, or else you will be trapped in the Underworld forever." Cyrus added, "Why don't you go up to your room and get your backpack. Bring along anything you think will be helpful."

Chance liked that idea quite a bit, as he always felt better when he brought some of his stuff along on any trip. Chance stopped one last time in front of Grant and touched the stone creature's knee for good luck.

In his room, Chance studied his belongings. He took a sweater, a flashlight, some rope, a compass, a pair of pliers, some wire, and his Swiss army knife. From the kitchen he grabbed a handful of granola bars and a bottle of water. Then he saw it—duct tape! Absolutely! Duct tape could fix anything. He grabbed the roll and held it high, as if this was a magic tape that would guarantee his safe return.

Just then Blixx walked in. "Ohhh, you are wise, young Magusss. I have read on the Internet that duct tape has hundredsss of usesss."

"We'll see, Blixx. I doubt anyone ever brought duct tape to the Underworld before. Just stick close by me once we're there, okay?"

Chance saw Bluthher in a corner of the kitchen, anxiously rubbing here hands on her apron. Not sure what to say, Chance waved good-bye to her, then left with Blixx out the back door. She waved back silently, and the last sight Chance took with him was her eyes welling up with tears.

Chance and Blixx walked the dark streets

CHAPTER SEVEN

The Goth-Beasts Attack

That night, Chance and Blixx walked through the dark streets north of Old Town. Blixx was dressed in one of Chance's sweatshirts rolled up jeans, and his lucky baseball cap. He held a carved stone Object of Power that glowed brighter as they walked north.

"Almossst there… almossst there. Yesss, very clossse."

Chance kept glancing behind them, staring into the shadows. He had the distinct feeling that they were being followed, but every time he checked back there, he saw nothing.

"Hey—pay attention, we're coming up to it now," Blixx hissed.

Chance glanced at the dark street behind him one last time, then turned around and kept walking.

Fifty feet behind them, Holly and Hayden peered around the corner of a building. Holly had earlier convinced Hayden that Chance was in trouble. Then they hid outside the museum for hours until Chance and Blixx snuck out.

"Get a load of that funny little guy holding the glowing thing," Hayden observed. "Must be one of those fluorescent night sticks, huh?"

"I don't know. This whole thing is so Hairy. Wonder what they're looking for?" Holly grew more anxious the longer they followed Chance. She wasn't concerned about her own safety; she could handle herself quite well. But Chance, well, he was a nice guy and all, but he was such a wimp. She just didn't want to see him get hurt, that's all.

As Chance rounded a corner, he and Blixx quickly ducked into the shadows. In the middle of the street, Sehti and five of his strange Goth-Beasts stood in front of the newly forming Rift.

"Hey, I thought he'd be alone!" Chance whispered.

"Ooh, looks like Sssehti's been busy. Let's just see what happens."

Sehti instructed his followers to stand guard. Then he stepped through the Rift and disappeared.

Blixx looked at Chance. "Ya better clobber dossse guysss wit yer Heka, kid."

"Yeah... uhh, right." Chance felt his confidence drain away. "Here goes nothing." He rolled up his sleeves to expose the Anubis Tape. "I'll use the Formulae that freezes them." He recited the Words of Power.

Nothing happened, and Chance began to panic. Then his Amulet glowed and a green shaft of light shot out and harmlessly struck the five creatures. They whirled at the disturbance, saw Chance and Blixx, and charged forward, snarling and growling.

"That wasn't supposed to happen," Chance cried.

"What did you do, boss? Run fer it!"

Both of them turned and pounded down the street. Chance desperately tried to remember his lesson with Cyrus. "It should have worked. Why didn't it work!?"

"Ya didn't sssay the wordssss right. Keep running!"

One of the creatures, the Goth-Cat, bounded forward and swiped at Chance's leg. As he ran, Blixx knocked over a trashcan right in front of the beast. It leapt high in the air over the can, landed on all fours, raised its head, and howled a horrible, bone-chilling cry.

"We're gonna die!" Blixx yelled.

"Stop yelling. I'm trying to think!"

"Over here." Blixx suddenly ran into an alley. "Follow me!"

But after a few steps, they realized the alley was a dead end. The Goth-Beasts followed them and blocked the only way out.

"Great!" Chance snapped. "Now we're trapped. Nice going, hose-head!"

"I didn't know it was a dead end! It's not my fault." Blixx moaned. "Do something, Chance!"

Meanwhile, Holly and Hayden weren't far behind. As they neared the alley, Holly grabbed an empty bottle off the ground and hurled it at the last Goth-Beast.

"Are you crazy?" Hayden yelled.

The bottle struck the back of the Goth-Beast's head. It turned, revealing small, close-set red eyes, a broad snout, and large tusks jutting up from his mouth. The man-beast squealed and charged at Holly and Hayden.

Let's get out of here!" Hayden yelled.

Although Holly thought she could take him, she knew she had to draw some of the goons away from Chance. "Look at his face," she shouted as they turned and ran. "He must be wearing a pig mask."

Back in the alley, Chance and Blixx slowly backed against the wall. The four remaining Goth-Beasts spread out into a line across the mouth of the alley. The Goth-Snake opened its jaws and a long forked tongue darted out, the Goth-Dog bared his long dripping fangs, the Goth-Cat flexed its long razor-sharp claws, and the Goth-Crocodile snorted and snarled.

"Try it again," Blixx yelled, grabbing Chance by the jacket. "We're trapped! You can do it. Just concentrate!"

Chance held out his hands and repeated the Formulae. It still didn't work.

"Wait." Blixx yelled. "I can hear Osirius talking to me… you left out the last letter "A".

"Oh yeah! The A! Okay, Blixx, stand back."

The Goth-Beasts all crouched at the same time and leapt at them just as Chance spread out his fingers and recited the Formulae. His Amulet glowed bright red, and the Anubis Tape vibrated and transformed into two armored shells around his arms. A red sphere shot out from Chance's hands and burst into a bright light.

The four Goth-Beasts froze in mid-air.

"You da man! I knew you could do it," Blixx

The four Goth-Beasts froze in mid-air

walked over to the Goth-Crocodile and kicked it.

"Let's get out of here!" Chance yelled, "I don't know how long they'll stay like that."

Meanwhile, the Goth-Pig was gaining on Holly and Hayden. "We've got to stop running and fight," Holly said, "or he'll catch us eventually."

"Uh—okay." Hayden didn't sound very enthusiastic about the whole idea. Holly shook her head. Boys, she thought.

They skidded to a stop near the back of a restaurant. There were trashcans, dumpsters, and crates lining both sides of the alley. Holly suddenly had an idea.

"Hayden—open that dumpster lid and get ready to slam it shut."

Holly grabbed a nearby trashcan lid, turned, and hurled it like a Frisbee. It struck the Goth-Pig in the face, breaking off one of its long slimy tusks. It clapped a hairy hand to its face and screamed in pain and rage.

Holly grabbed another trashcan lid to use as a shield. She jumped on a crate, then leaped to the outer lip of the dumpster. It was rounded and narrower than the balance beam she used in gymnastics class and she struggled to stay balanced.

“C’mon, pigface. Come and get me.” Holly waved her arms, taunting the Goth-pig. The creature leapt at her, almost catching Holly by surprise. At the last second, she jumped off the edge, hit the pavement, and rolled into a somersault. The Goth-Pig sailed into the wall, then fell right in the dumpster with a loud crash! Hayden quickly flipped over the metal lid.

But the Goth-Pig was already trying to escape his makeshift prison. Hayden jumped on top, using his weight to keep the clattering lid down. As he struggled to keep it closed, Holly was suddenly there and she locked the metal clasp onto the latch. Hayden jumped off the dumpster and hugged her.

“You were awesome, Holly. What a team!”

"C'mon, Hayden, we gotta help Chance. He's got four more of these goons chasing him."

They turned and ran down the street in search of Chance, leaving the Goth-Pig battering the walls of the dumpster, its angry snarls echoing through the alley.

The Eternity Bridge stretched ahead of them

CHAPTER EIGHT

The Underworld is No Place for the Faint of Heart

Chance and Blixx ran back to the swirling Rift. They looked at each other, then back at the gateway between worlds.

"Um, I don't sssuppose you've ever done thisss before, have you?" Blixx asked Chance.

"No, I was just about to ask you the same question," Chance replied as that uneasy feeling returned in his stomach. *Heck, in my whole body*, he thought. He thought of his father again, lost somewhere in Limbo, and remembered a favorite saying that he told Chance all the time.

"When you cannot go back, then you can only go forward," Chance muttered.

"What's dat you sssaid?"

"Nothing, Blixx. Come on, let's go."

Chance took a deep breath and stepped through the opening, followed closely by Blixx.

The very next step they took was in the Underworld—a desolate landscape of gnarled, twisted rock and swirling blue-green mist. Nothing was alive, not even a single bird, insect, plant, or patch of moss, not the tiniest speck of life. Only barren, tortured stone

The Eternity Bridge, a huge soaring arch of thousands of stone blocks, stretched just ahead of them over the River of Souls. It looked very old, as if it had stood there since the beginning of time. Chance was breathless with anxiety realizing that he stood in the place he had dreaded so much. To make matters worse, when he looked back, he realized he could not see the opening of the Rift. He felt his panic rising, and tried to keep calm as he looked for it.

"Where's the Rift, Blixx?"

"Don't ya worry none, master. I know da way."

"Oh yeah? Show me."

Looking hurt, Blixx walked back a few feet and stuck his hand out. It disappeared up to his elbow. "Sssee. Told ya. Now do you trust me?"

"Okay. I'm sorry. I'm a little bit—okay, a lot nervous. We'd better get going, Sehti is probably way ahead of us by now." Chance hoped he sounded confident; he didn't want Blixx to notice that he was trembling.

They stepped onto the bridge. Chance's eyes widened when he saw that many stone blocks were missing from the floor. Looking down, he saw the river underneath, except it didn't look like a river at all. Against his better judgment, Chance walked to the side of the bridge and looked over. Instead of water, the river was made of a gleaming blue translucent fog that contained millions of human figures crowded like schools of fish, drifting with the ebbs and flows of the currents.

Chance heard whispering voices begging to be saved, begging him to reach down and lift them out. They cried out in agony, the mouths opening like deep holes. The chorus of whispers grew louder and louder. *"Help me... Save me... Free me"* Chance wanted to turn away and keep going on the bridge, but his feet wouldn't move. He wanted to cry out, but his lips were sealed shut.

"Hey, bossss, thisss is no time to go fissshing." Blixx pulled at Chances arm. "C'mon—let's go!"

Chance snapped out of the spell. The river was empty; there were no bodies, no faces below.

"Uhhh, Blixx, do you see anything down there?"

Blixx looked down. "Nope. Wait…is that a

Chance looked over the side of the bridge

fissshy? No… guesss not."

"And you didn't hear anything?"

"I don't hear nothing'" Blixx looked up at Chance with a frown. "Yer ssstartin' ta sssspook me, kid. Let's get goin'"

Though Chance was hardly athletic, he ran across the bridge faster than he had ever run before. *Maybe even faster than Holly,* he thought as they reached the other side in record time.

The Underworld landscape stretched out before him. There were bottomless black pits scattered all over the ground. Countless rocks of all sizes and shapes drifted aimlessly in the sky. It wasn't hot or cold, it just felt—neutral, neither good or bad.

"Wow, the first level of the Underworld," Chance said softly.

"The ancient scrolls call this the Level of Eternal Emptiness," Blixx added. "Now I know why."

Chance tried to reach out with his mind like Cyrus had taught him, but he didn't feel Sehti's presence. And even worse, he didn't sense his father's Ka anywhere.

"Hey bossss, ya hear that?" Blixx tugged on his pant leg. Chance quit trying to sense anything and listened. Sure enough, he heard a strange growling noise in the distance.

Chance gulped. "Okay, let's check that out—carefully."

Blixx and he crept forward until they saw two

hideous monsters that had trapped Sehti against a boulder. Each creature's body consisted of a huge, misshapen head. Instead of ears, multi-jointed legs jutted out. Two fifteen foot long reptilian tails extended from what would have been the back of their necks and slapped the ground. Chance was sure Sehti was doomed.

The creatures lunged. Sehti tore a length of the Anubis Tapestry from his arm and held it between his outstretched hands, chanting Words of Power. The section of Tape glowed bright red and the monsters were instantly surrounded by a swirling tornado of blue mist that lifted them high into the sky.

Sehti rewrapped the Anubis Tape around his arm and strode forward. All dressed in black, the Tape writhing about his head, Sehti definitely looked like the Lord of the Underworld. The idea of confronting a being of such tremendous power seemed ridiculous to Chance. *I must have been nuts to think I could do this by myself.*

“Blixx, are you in contact with Cyrus?” Chance asked his sidekick as they followed Sehti from a safe distance. “If you are, tell him he’s crazy if he thinks I can take Sehti on alone!”

Blixx concentrated and wrinkled his brow. “You betcha. I can hear his thoughts. He said you are doing fine. And… something about don’t forget the rock spell.”

Chance didn't feel any better. He didn't know what Cyrus could have said to ease his fears, but he would have welcomed something profound. He tried again to make his mind reach out to find his father's spirit, but he felt nothing. Chance pulled out the Heka Hourglass. It was a quarter empty already.

Ahead of them, Sehti turned and walked into a narrow fissure in a cliff wall. Chance and Blixx quickened their pace. As they stood in front of the tight space, Chance's worries grew. It was very dark in there, and they would be extremely vulnerable once they started inside. They slowly entered, Chance first, with Blixx following right behind. Chance felt Blixx trembling, and a part of him was relieved that the little creature was afraid too.

Suddenly Sehti stopped. Chance quickly whispered the Formulae that changed their appearance into a rock just as, Sehti swirled around and stared in their direction. Chance and Blixx held their breath. Sehti walked towards them and stopped so close that Chance saw the red veins in the Heka-Priest's eyes as the undead warrior stared straight at him. Blixx squeezed Chance's arm so tight he had to bite his lip, or else he would cry out in pain.

After what seemed like an eternity, Sehti turned around and walked into the darkness ahead. Chance pried Blixx's fingers loose and breathed a sigh of relief.

"Next time, grab your own arm and squeeze it, not mine, you big baby."

"Sssorry, boss." Blixx said, dropping his head in shame. "I thought our number wassss up."

Yeah, so did I, Chance thought, but didn't say, not wanting to scare Blixx any more.

They separated and instantly the rock illusion disappeared. They followed Sehti until he stopped in front of an arched rock formation with strange carvings on it that looked like Symbols of Power. Like the bridge, it also looked much older than all the rock nearby. Then Chance realized what he was looking at—it was the first portal!

"That's it, bossss, Blixx whispered. They call it the Portal of Shadows."

Sehti looked about, knowing that the monster that guards the portal would soon strike. Planting his legs wide, he threw his arms out to his side. "Show yourself, demon. I command you by your name—Blauster-op-teh!"

A being that Chance could only describe as horrible peeled itself away from the canyon wall. It was a misshapen thing at least twelve feet tall, with no neck or head, just a large square torso with a pair of small sinewy arms, and two powerful lumpy legs. In the center of its body was a huge single eye that squinted angrily at Sehti.

Sehti waved his hands and recited a Formulae. Yellow streaks of light shot out from his fingertips and struck the guardian. The creature howled in pain and threw its tiny hands in front of its face, then froze in place where it stood, just like Chance had done to the Goth-Beasts back home. Without a second glance, Sehti walked past the motionless beast and into the portal where his body shimmered momentarily, and then vanished.

Seconds later, the monster unfroze and angrily looked around the crevasse.

"Hey, why don'tcha use yer freezin' spell again?" Blixx whispered.

Chance softly spoke the Formulae, pronouncing every syllable precisely. The monster's legs froze, but not its upper body. Its hands furiously pounded against its legs until it broke free of Chance's spell. The beast crouched, threw its arms back and jutted its torso forward, its eye peering into the darkness.

"Great," Blixx gulped. "I guess da spell don't work so good on dese monstersssss." He looked at Chance, his lower lip quivering. "Ya gotta try something else. What about the duct tape?"

Chance mentally ran down the list of the precious few spells he knew. Maybe the rock disguise could fool it! "I've got an idea, Blixx. Whatever you do, just stay with me."

Chance repeated the rock Formulae, and the rock disguise appeared around them. As soon as the Guardian looked away from them, Chance and

Blixx took several steps forward. The lumpy beast glanced back in their direction. They stopped. The second it turned away they took several more steps forward. When the monster turned back in their direction, Chance and Blixx again stood still. They repeated this maneuver again. The monster swung back to look right at them and stepped towards them suspiciously; its one brow furrowed in what passed for deep thought.

"Uh oh," Chance whispered, "I think it's on to us."

"Do something!"

"Why don't YOU do something? What good are you anyway?"

"I'm the one who knowsss da way outta here," Blixx grumbled with great indignation. "I do one thing, and I do it very well."

The lumpy monster, now only a few feet away, turned to the canyon wall and ripped off a large chunk of rock to smash Chance and Blixx with. The big, awful eye in the middle of the creature's chest squinted at Chance as if it could see through

The monster ripped apart a large chunk of rock

the rock illusion.

Chance didn't know of any Heka magick that would help, but maybe something in his backpack would be useful. He unzipped it and rummaged around. "Let's see, I've got Duct Tape, granola bar, flash light, army knife… Wait! My flashlight—what if it was the light from Sehti's spell that froze the monster? It is dark in here, and the monster doesn't have an eyelid. I wonder…"

"Whatever you're gonna do, do it fast! Blixx wailed.

Chance looked up to see the monster raising the boulder to drop on the two of them. He grabbed his flashlight, hit the switch, and shined the light directly into the big eyeball. The monster froze while holding the boulder high overhead.

"Ya did it! Ya did it!" Blixx exclaimed.

"Yeah, I did, didn't I? Wow! How about that? That's one of the coolest things I've ever done in my whole life. Now let's get out of here."

Leaving the monster frozen behind them, they ran as fast as they could into the portal.

Stepping through the portal

CHAPTER NINE

Showdown with Sehti

Chance and Blixx stepped out onto the second level of the Underworld. Looking across the lifeless landscape, Chance noted how similar it was to the first level except for the red colors in the rocks and the purple mist.

"Don't you forget where the portal is, Blixx!"

"I told you—I do one thing, and I do it very well."

"Yeah, so you said. For both our sakes, you'd better be right." Chance looked left and right, trying to decide which way to go. He noticed that large boulders littered the terrain for as far as the eye could see. “Hey, Blixxx, it’s a lot rockier here, isn’t it?”

“Thisss is the Level of Thundering Rocksss. But, don’t asssk me what that means.”

“Thundering Rocks. I don’t like the sound of that.”

Chance again looked at the Heka Hourglass. It didn’t seem possible, but the glass chamber was now half empty. Chance was really nervous—he no longer had a sense of the passage of time. Were minutes passing, or hours, or just seconds? He would have to constantly check the Hourglass to know when to start back.

Chance tried concentrating on Sehti again, but after a minute of trying to probe with his mind, he felt nothing. Cyrus had said that his blood-link with Sehti would be an advantage, so why wasn’t it working? Chance suddenly had a strange idea.

He took his Swiss army knife out of his pocket and poked his left thumb. A tiny drop of blood formed. He held his left hand out, closed his eyes, and concentrated. Chance began to feel something out there—a presence, like his own, of his same blood, that was close—very close. He looked about the desolate landscape.

"I can feel Sehti somewhere nearby… but I can't see him."

Blixx looked around. He tapped Chance on the shoulder and pointed straight up. "If he is closssse by, he mussst be up there, don't ya think, bosss?"

Chance looked up at the floating rocks. "Blixx, you're definitely smarter than you look."

"Why… thanksss. I didn't think it ssshowed. My mother alwaysss told me…" Chance was already walking towards a cliff wall. "Hey, wait fer me!"

Climbing up the rocky cliff was one of the hardest things Chance had ever done. Fortunately Blixx was a natural climber, saving Chance from a horrible fall several times. They finally reached the top where they could look out across the floating boulders. Far away, they heard rumbling, growling thunder that sometimes sounded like crashing, or colliding rocks. *I definitely don't like the sound of that,* Chance thought.

After getting his breath back, Chance closed his eyes and tried to sense his father's spirit somewhere in the vast wasteland. He didn't even know if the Ka was on this level at all or whether it could travel from one level to another. Again he came up empty. Chance dreaded the idea of returning home empty handed, and leaving his father trapped in the void forever.

Pulling the Talisman out of his backpack, Chance held it over his head, hoping that the Heka Figure of Power might attract his father's Ka like a magnet. But still… nothing happened.

"Look!" Blixx yelled. "I see Sehti on that large red boulder!"

Chance was confused. Should he go after Sehti or continue searching for his father? He rubbed the talisman affectionately and tried to imagine what his father would say. He'd say *I have to go after Sehti, to stop him from taking over the world,* that's what he'd say. He clenched his teeth with grim determination and reluctantly put the Talisman back into his backpack.

"C'mon, boss. We've got work to do."

Chance was too choked up to talk; he just nodded.

As they jumped from boulder to boulder they

They jumped from boulder to boulder

saw Sehti fighting something in the middle of the large floating rock where the second portal stood. Sehti hurled a spell at a big round monster that sent it ricocheting off the rocks like a rubber ball. The creature was weakened, but still full of fight. It growled and opened its mouth to reveal horrible rows of long razor sharp teeth. Sehti chanted another Formulae. The creature spun around like a large, toothy top, and quickly lost consciousness. Sehti stepped into the portal and disappeared.

Chance and Blixx jumped onto the boulder and cautiously walked past the fallen monster. Chance noticed it had ridiculously tiny arms and legs that were almost hidden by a thick coat of long silky brown hair. "So, what do you call this thing, Blixx?"

"It's Phtha-hak, guardian of the Floating Portal."

"If you knew they called it the Floating Portal, you could have told me earlier. It would have been easier to find, you dummy."

"Oh yeah… umm… I sssee what ya…"

Suddenly Sehti stepped out of the portal! Chance and Blixx froze in terror.

"I thought I was being followed. Just as you could sense me, I can sense you, Chance Henry." Sehti looked at Blixx with amusement. "And what do we have here… an Ihhmph? How quaint. Not very useful, but still… an entertaining companion, in its way. But now you will be a dead companion!"

Sehti casually hurled a bright green bolt of

light at Blixx. Chance didn't think, he simply reacted and threw himself in front of the cowering sidekick, taking the full brunt of the spell. The two landed in a heap. To Chance's surprise, he was unharmed. Blixx wrapped his spindly arms around Chance, momentarily blocking his sight. Chance struggled to push Blixx away, trying to see what Sehti was going to do.

"Blixx, get off me!"

Suddenly Sehti screeched in agony. All of the Symbols on his Anubis Tape glowed bright red, and black smoke drifted from his hands. Chance recoiled in horror.

"Curse the laws of Heka! Woe be to one who would strike another of the same blood. Agghhh… the PAIN!!"

Chance slowly understood what had happened. By throwing himself in front of Blixx, he caused Sehti's violent attack to fall on him, which, as Cyrus had told him, was a violation of the ancient laws of Heka. With great difficulty, Sehti stood on shaky legs. Was it Chance's imagination, or did

Suddenly Sehti screamed a screeching cry of agony

Sehti seem smaller now? And thinner?

"Noooo. By the Old Ones, do not punish me. Do not take away my strength! The boy… the boy tricked me."

Seizing the moment, Chance stood, pointed his fingertips at the Magus, and recited the Formulae that would freeze him. Yellow discs of light formed around each hand, then streaks of light shot through the air.

Sehti threw his arms out, crossed his wrists, and deflected the yellow streaks upwards.

"Don't tell me that's all Osirius has taught you?" Sehti sneered. "Oh how you will pay for the lessening of my powers. I may never again be strong enough to return to the Underworld and defeat Anubis, but I have many times the power I need to trap you here forever."

"Hey, boss." Blixx tapped Chance on the shoulder. "Maybe you should try the flashlight. Or maybe… the duct tape?"

"Blixx, would you please be quiet? We're fighting for our lives!"

Blixx's ears suddenly perked up as he heard a crack of thunder, and he looked up to the sky. "Uh oh… we got more problems."

Chance looked up and saw that his deflected spell had crashed into several floating boulders. They were colliding with other boulders the chain reaction of collisions was escalating. But Chance didn't have time to think about this new problem.

Sehti lifted his foot and stomped it on the ground. The resulting shockwave split open a crevice in the ground that snaked towards Chance and Blixx. They jumped to the side just as the ground where they had been standing split apart.

"Pathetic." Sehti hissed. "Osirius had no right to send a boy to do a man's work. You have failed, Chance Henry. You've failed Osirius, and all humanity. But most of all, you've failed your father."

Chance's head snapped up, his face red with anger. "You don't know anything about my father. If he were here, he'd tell you so."

"Oh, my young friend, he is indeed here,

closer than you could know. And he will be here for eternity."

Just then it dawned on Chance that if Sehti knew where his father's Ka was, he could bring it to them. Could Chance be so clever…that he could trick Sehti?

"Dad? Dad, are you here? Tell him…tell Sehti he's wrong!" Chance tried to act like he was nearly hysterical, which wasn't too difficult, under the circumstances. "DAD!! Where are you?"

"Yes, I imagine you would like to talk with him one last time" Sehti said, grinning like a wolf at Chance's emotional outburst. "It would please me to add to your anguish, to let you speak to your father, knowing you will never see him again. Here, then, young Henry, is your father—for the last time!"

Sehti placed his fingertips on his temple and concentrated. His features became softer, gentler, more like the face of Chance's father.

"Chaaaaaance…" said the face of George Henry. "Do what you must to save yourself. Don't ever forget that I love you, and always will."

Sehti pulled away his fingertips. His face twisted into a grotesque smile.

"Hahahhaaa! There you have it, little man—the last goodbye." He paused. "Hmmm, I think I'll leave you with one last gift." Sehti waved his hands over his head, then pointed at Blixx.

The little creature screwed up his face like he was concentrating hard on something. "Boss—I don't hear Ossiriusss' thoughtsss anymore."

"Quite right, little Ihhmph. I have severed your connection. You are now alone—hopelessly, completely alone. Enjoy eternity," Sehti said as he leapt to an adjacent floating rock. "Remember, the first ten thousand years is only just the beginning. Ha ha ha ha!"

Sehti jumped to another boulder, then turned and destroyed the first boulder with a spell. Then he jumped to the next boulder, and again destroyed the previous one. He weakened, then staggered as he struggled to continue. He destroyed two more boulders, until there were no close rocks for

Chance and Blixx to jump to.

It was also obvious to Chance that Sehti was having difficulty. It didn't occur to him that in defeating Sehti, he might have inadvertently caused the permanent destruction of his father. For now, he only felt hope—he knew his dad's Ka was nearby.

"This has got to work," Chance said as he tore open his backpack and pulled out the Talisman. "Dad's nearby now, he's got to be!"

Holding the Talisman in both hands, he recited the Formulae Cyrus had taught him. The Talisman shivered in his grip and started to glow. Chance watched eagerly as the Talisman slowly grew to a height of twelve inches. The glow faded. Chance brought the Talisman close to his face, examining it.

"Blixx, I think… I think it worked! Cyrus said that the Talisman would grow if my father's Ka was pulled inside. He's in there; I can feel it. It worked!"

But the joy of celebration quickly faded as

a boulder collided with the rock they stood on causing a large chunk to break off. Then another rock struck the ground only five feet from where they stood. The roars of thunder grew louder with each passing second.

"Blixx, how are we going to get out of here? We're running out of time!"

Chance took out the Hourglass. It was almost empty! They looked over the edge of the boulder and saw that they were at least a hundred feet above the ground. Chance looked for anything that might help them, but saw nothing.

"Bossss, what about the duct tape? It can sssave us, you will sssee."

"Blixx, if you say one more thing about duct tape, I'll strangle you.

A large boulder fell from above and struck the boulder with a deafening blast of thunder. Almost half of the ground broke apart and drifted away. More of the fracture point was crumbling and soon there would be little left of the boulder to stand on. And still the thunder grew louder

Chance felt a rising wave of uncontrollable anger and fear surge through him. Out of sheer frustration, he walked over to the motionless monster and kicked it. The creature rolled several feet, struck a rock, bounced three feet in the air, and tumbled back to Chance. Blixx walked over and looked at it, a thoughtful expression on his face. Chance and he looked at each other and nodded.

Several more small rocks fell from above, striking the area near Chance and Blixx.

They rolled the monster to the edge of the boulder. It growled softly, but didn't wake up. Chance and Blixx pushed the beast over the edge and jumped on its back, holding onto the long silky hair.

They fell much too fast for Chance's liking, hit the ground, and bounced high up into the sky. The creature was slowly regaining consciousness. Its growling intensified and its body quivered. Chance and Blixx were flung wildly about but they held on for dear life.

They bounced several more times, each arc

lower than before. By now the creature was awake, but it's tiny arms couldn't reach around to grab the two unwelcome riders. It roared ferociously and snapped it's jaws hungrily.

"What happens when we stop bouncing?" Blixx asked. "It will kill usss fer sssure"

Chance looked down and saw several deep pits nearby. "Lean to your left. Let's try and steer the direction of our next bounce. Get ready to jump!"

They leaned to the side. When the monster hit the ground they jumped off. Their shift in weight had changed the trajectory of the bouncing, so when the monster rebounded ten feet in the air and then fell again, it dropped into a deep pit.

Although congratulations were definitely in order, instead Chance and Blixx ran as fast as they could to the portal to level one. Without breaking stride, they jumped through and landed in the first level. The monster in the dark crevasse stepped aside in obedience because Chance had defeated it earlier. As they ran past, Chance felt a tiny shiver of excitement at being able to command such a terrible creature.

Another look at the Hourglass revealed that almost all the sands had fallen through—it was almost twilight in Portland. Chance clutched the timepiece and ran even faster, breathing so hard he thought his lungs would burst.

Son they reached the Eternity Bridge. They zigzagged across the walkway, avoiding the holes above the River of Souls.

"Don't look down," Blixx huffed. He was also breathing hard, and his big, hairy head glistened with sweat.

"You don't have to tell me that again."

As they left the bridge, Chance slowed to a trot. "Okay, Blixx, do your thing…the one thing you do so well."

Blixx turned and saluted as he ran. "Your wish is my…" He tripped on a rock, hit the ground hard, and lay motionless.

"Blixx! BLIXX! Don't do this to me." Chance sat him upright and shook him. "Wake up! WE'RE OUT OF TIME!!" Chance looked at the Hourglass. Precious few grains of sand remained.

Chance panicked. They were so close. Now what? He ran in circles, his hands outstretched, groping in the air, hoping he could find the Rift.

"It's gotta be here somewhere. Where is it? WHERE IS IT?"

Chance realized what a fool he had been. It was hopeless! He was, after all, only a kid—a stupid fool for even thinking he could pull this off. For a while, he thought he was really special. But this was reality—and he was doomed!

"WAKE UP!! BLIXX—WAKE UP!!" Chance grabbed Blixx and shook him hard. "WHERE IS

THE RIFT? It's inside your head somewhere, if I could just reach in there and… grab… it!"

Chance paused. "Hey… maybe I can." He remembered when Cyrus had first held his head and read his mind to learn English. Now that Chance wore the Anubis Tapestry, why couldn't he do it as well?

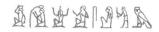

Chance held Blixx's head and concentrated. Nothing happened. He tried again, reaching out as hard as he could. The symbols on the Anubis Tape glowed and he felt himself falling, falling into Blixx's thoughts, their minds joining. Chance saw everything Blixx had seen in the Underworld from the time they had first entered.

Chance knew the Rift was eighty feet straight ahead.

He let go of Blixx's head and tried to lift him, but the Ihhmph was too heavy. "How can someone so small weigh so much?" Chance dared not look at the Hourglass. In his mind he could see the last grains of sand rolling around in a smaller and smaller circle, ready to drop through at any moment.

"I'm not leaving without you, Blixx! Unnhhh… come on!"

Lifting Blixx under his shoulders, Chance dragged him, foot by painful foot. Chance was drenched with sweat and his heart pounded. Chance wanted to go home so bad. He dug deep, deeper than he had ever thought was possible, and tried again, pulling and tugging Blixx's dead weight.

"Come on… COME ON!! ALMOST THERE!" Chance didn't know who he was shouting at, Blixx or himself, but it seemed to work, as he pulled

Chance dragged him, foot by painful foot

Blixx forward with all the strength he had left.

Suddenly they were through the Rift. As sson as his feet hit the pavement, Chance held up the Hourglass and saw one last grain of sand fall through the narrow opening into the bottom pile. The sky was pink with the first blush of dawning twilight.

Blixx bolted upright. “Owww, my poor little head. What happened? Hey! We’re back! We made it. How did…?” A look of realization and amazement played across his face. “It was the duct tape, wasn’t it?”

“Yeah, Blixx. It was the duct tape.” Chance smiled and shook his head and walked away. “The Duct Tape brought us back.”

EPILOGUE

Chance delicately placed the Talisman on the warehouse table. Excitement flooded through him now that Cyrus would be able to bring his father back to life. Cyrus beamed with pleasure.

Next to him, the mummy beamed with pleasure. "Congratulations, Chance. From what you've told me, I believe Sehti will never again gain access to the Rift between Twilights. I was right about you all along."

"I was right too," Blixx added. "Didn't I say he would be a great Magus?"

"Thanks," Chance said humbly. "It was all so amazing. I feel so—different now." And he did feel different, more confident than he had ever been. He had faced the Underworld and survived—and, almost more importantly, he had brought his father's Ka back as well.

"You hold on to those feelings, Chance." Cyrus put his hands on Chance's shoulders. "You've earned the right to them."

"I don't think I can wait another moment," Chance said. "Go ahead, Uncle Cy. Bring back my father."

A sad look came over Cyrus's face, and Chance frowned when he saw it.

"Well, Chance, you see… it's a bit more complicated than that. We still must find and defeat Sehti so that we can return your father's Ka into its original body. I firmly believe—"

"No! No, Cyrus." Chance felt like he'd been kicked in the stomach. "You said… you said if I brought my father's Ka back, he could be saved. You said so. You promised!"

"I'm sorry, Chance. It's disappointing, I know. You did have to bring back the Ka to save your father. Without it there would be no hope. But we still have much more work to do." Cyrus studied the Talisman. "It is possible, though, to now communicate with your father."

"I thought you were being honest with me." scowled. "You just told me what you wanted me to hear." Suddenly a dark thought crossed his mind. "Wait a minute. What would happen if Sehti didn't make it out of the Underworld before twilight? What if he died there? It would be all my fault. My fault, that… we couldn't… save dad. Cyrus… what can we do?"

"There is no point in fearing the worst. I will use the Pyramid of Power and consult with the Vestige to try and learn of Sehti's fate. Please, Chance, you must not…"

Just then, they heard a crashing sound. Cyrus changed into his human form and ran through the warehouse door. When Chance caught up, Cyrus was holding Holly by her jacket. Standing behind Holly in a corner were Hayden and Christie.

"Chance... help!" Holly yelled as she struggled to break free.

"What are you kids doing in here?" Cyrus asked. "It is against the law to trespass!"

"We saw everything. We saw a mummy, and a little strange animal... and a giant statue," Holly admitted."

"We were worried about you," Hayden added. "Holly and I followed you tonight in Old Town and we ran into this pig-guy that was attacking you. We just wanted to see if you were okay, that's all. Honest!"

"If you're in trouble," Christie chimed in, "we can help. We're you're friends, aren't we? C'mon, Chance—we're the Horde!"

"I'm not sure what to do about this," Cyrus said. "Erasing memories is extremely difficult. This is very serious. We can't let our secret out."

"But we can keep a secret." Holly pleaded.

"We've always trusted each other."

"Chance, would you trust these three with your life?" Cyrus asked. "Would you trust them with the fate of all humanity?"

"All humanity?" Hayden gasped.

Chance took a moment to look at his friends in the light of the past few days. Even dangling off the ground, Holly looked ready to kick someone, so he knew she was ready. Hayden and Christie were both standing behind Cyrus and her, their faces set. He knew what his answer would be.

"Yes, Cyrus," Chance said, smiling at his friends. "Yes, I would trust them all."

"So be it." Cyrus transformed back into his mummy appearance, causing the other three members of the Horde to gasp.

They all walked into the warehouse, where Cyrus and Chance briefly explained the events of the last few days. Every now and then Chance's friends looked at Cyrus, Grant or Blixx in utter amazement.

"I think it's time to dissolve the partnership

of the Horde," Holly announced at the end of the explanation, "and create a new partnership. We need a new name."

"My dad is an attorney," Christie said, "and he talks a lot about his business, and I've heard him mention this thing called a Trust. It's something to do with people joining together to do something important. Well, isn't that what we're doing now? And…don't we have to trust each other more than ever before?"

For a moment they all were silent.

"I like it," Holly said.

"Let's all sign a… a uhh, a contract," Hayden added. "That makes it official."

If Cyrus had any remaining doubts, they were erased by the responsible manner in which the four friends formed a new partnership. Cyrus placed a sheet of Egyptian papyrus on the table, then drew a Symbol of Power on it. He poured cinnamon in a bowl and added water slowly, making a paste.

"This image holds great power," Cyrus explained, pointing at the paper. "Whoever places their thumbprint of cinnamon over it will be bound by the spiritual laws of honesty, integrity, and… truth."

Everyone in the room became solemn. One by one they placed their thumbs in the cinnamon and left their thumbprint over the Symbol of Power. Cyrus waved his hands over the papyrus and an orange vapor rose from it.

Everyone shook hands, including Cyrus. Chance was so excited to now have the help of his friends that he forget for the moment how disappointed he was with the mummy.

Then Chance heard a sound he'd only heard once before—a scraping of rocks. Chance felt suddenly chilled.

"Chance, what's wrong?" Holly asked. You look so pale all of a sudden."

Chance swung around and looked at Grant. Grant was motionless.

"Chance, are you all right?" Holly asked.

"I don't know, Holly. Maybe it's just my imagination. Everything is okay… I guess." But he knew that everything wasn't all right. Even though Cyrus hadn't consulted with the Pyramid of Power, Chase knew that Sehti had made it back to this world, and that they would meet again. *But not today,* he thought. He felt a nudge, and looked up at Holly.

"Earth to Henry, come in Henry. Now that we're all together again, there's nothing we can't do. So, tell us… tell us the whole story."

Chance looked again at Grant, then shrugged off his feeling of unease. After all that he'd been through, how could he ever be afraid again? He had been born anew, in the fires of adventure and danger.

And he had quite an amazing story to tell.

THE END

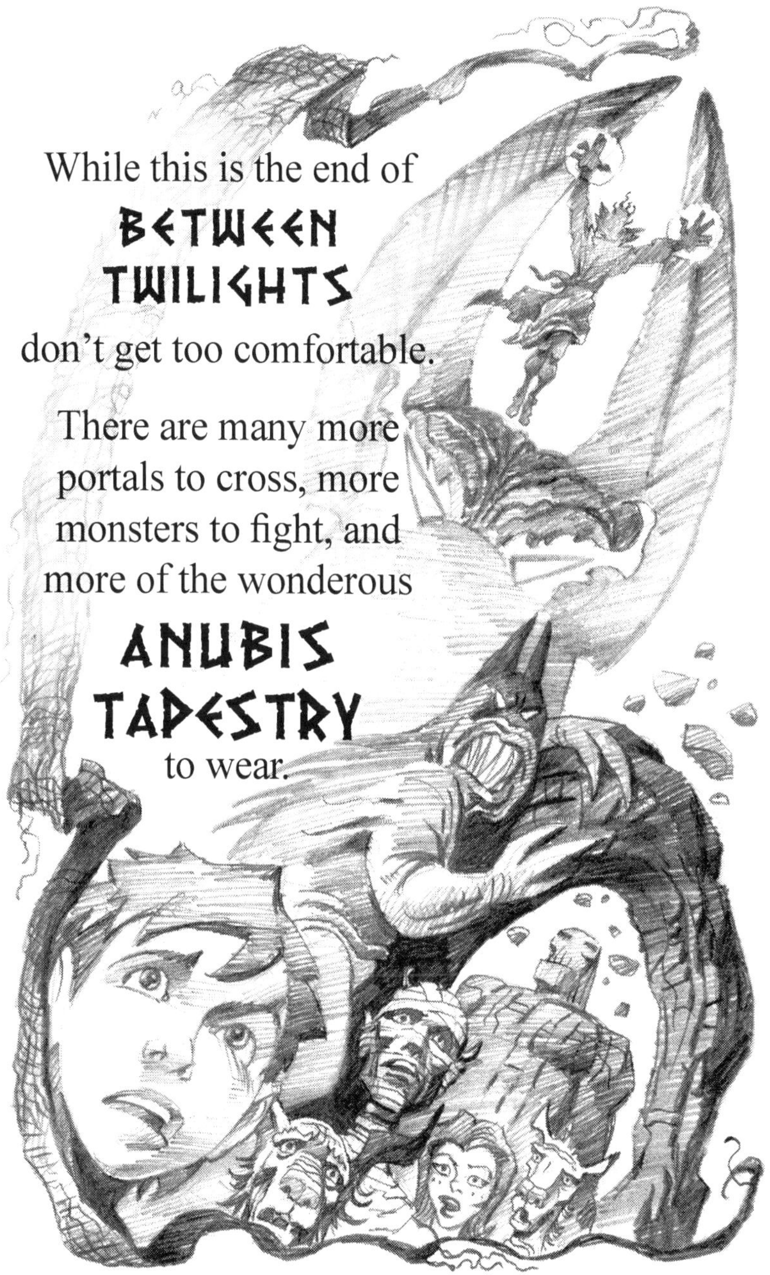
While this is the end of
BETWEEN TWILIGHTS
don't get too comfortable.
There are many more portals to cross, more monsters to fight, and more of the wonderous
ANUBIS TAPESTRY
to wear.

ACTIONOPOLIS

ABOUT THE AUTHOR

Bruce Zick has been writing and designing for Film, Animation, and Comic Book companies for 20 years, working for George Lucas, Steven Spielberg, Francis Ford Copolla, Disney, Pixar, Fox, Warner Bros., Marvel Comics, and Dark Horse Comics. Titles worked on include *Finding Nemo, A Bug's Life, Fantasia 2000, Valiant, Titan A.E., Tarzan, Hercules, Pocahontas, Lion King, Prince of Egypt, Road to El Dorado, Thor*, and many others. He has also sold two original film projects to 20th Century Fox.

BRUCE ZICK

ABOUT THE CREATOR

Shannon Eric Denton is an award winning storyteller. Shannon created ACTIONOPOLIS to actualize his ideas into a line of fast paced books for adventure lovers of any age. He has been fortunate to have worked professionally as an artist, writer, editor, director, and producer making comic books, children's books, Emmy nominated TV shows, Oscar nominated movies, toys and video games for studios such as Marvel, DC, Disney, WB, Fox, Lego, Sony, Nickelodeon, and Cartoon Network.

www.shannondenton.com
www.actionopolis.com
www.agentofdanger.com

ACTIONOPOLIS:

When Adventure Is Your Destination!

ABOUT THE CREATOR

Designer **Patrick Coyle**, along with Shannon Eric Denton, is the co-founder of the publishing company Komikwerks, LLC. Komikwerks publishes ebooks, graphic novels and novels for young adults. They have been lucky enough to publish the works of Ray Bradbury, Raymond Chandler, Joe Kubert, and Stan Lee among others. The Komikwerks graphic novel WORLD OF QUEST was optioned by Kids WB and ran for two seasons on the network. Komikwerks has been featured in many news and entertainment periodicals including Variety and USA Today.

30748884R00119

Made in the USA
Middletown, DE
08 April 2016